A Murder Unseen

A Murder Unseen

by
Rosie Cochran

Also by Rosie Cochran
Betrayed
Identity Revealed

© 2011 by Rosie Cochran. All rights reserved.

No part of this publication may be reproduced, stored in a retrieval system or transmitted in any way by any means—electronic, mechanical, photocopy, recording or otherwise—without the prior permission of the copyright holder, except as provided by USA copyright law.

Unless otherwise noted all scripture references are taken from the King James Version of the Bible.

Dedication

I dedicate this novel to the man who has been my best friend, a strong shoulder for me to lean on, my encourager, the one who keeps me balanced and makes me laugh—and the one person I never want to be without. I dedicate this book to my husband, Matt Cochran.

Special Thanks

To my sister, Gillian Lawrence, for her expertise and patience in assisting in the editing and proofreading of this novel, for her words of advice in areas of plot and consistency, but mostly, for being the best sister a woman could ask for.

Table of Contents

- The Witness 11
- A Family Trip 23
- The Cottage 31
- The Plan 37
- The Journey 43
- California 47
- Roger 51
- Discovered 63
- Secrets 77
- Questioned 93
- Discovered 97
- No Place to Hide 103
- My Name Is… 111
- Fingerprints Don't Lie 121
- The Safe House 133
- Fear 147
- Unacceptable Risk 155
- Reasonable Doubt 163
- Found! 173
- Shot 185
- Who Are You? 195
- Jon 207
- Let Us Help 217
- Shock 227

Escape 241
Loyalty 251
Meeting Candis.. 259
Good News! 271
Cleared 277

Chapter 1

The Witness

For a lady to take a shortcut through a dimly lit back alley close to midnight is not advisable. I should have known better. I did know better, but I was in a hurry. I was tired and not thinking clearly. It had been a long day at the hospital where I worked as a registered nurse. A double shift was not what I had planned on, but it was what I ended up working. All I wanted to do was to get home.

Home. What a wonderful ring that word held for me. Home was all about family. Home was where Henry was. Henry and my beloved children.

I was 23 when I met Henry. He was 26 and in his fourth year of medical school. Chance would have it that his clinical rotations were scheduled at the same hospital and on the same floor where I was working my first real job as a registered nurse. It wasn't love at first sight. Henry wasn't flashy like the men I had dated up until then, but he made me feel special and important. He was mature and stable. Stability was what I needed more than love, though love was still high on my list. When he reminded me of my father, whom I adored, I knew one day I would marry him.

I still grieve when I think of my father's early and unexpected death. A heart attack, they told me. He was so strong, so healthy. Then he was gone. And I? I was left an orphan since my mother died in childbirth with me.

But back to Henry. A few years later, I did marry him and not just because of his stability and maturity. I grew to love him with a true and deep love, not simple infatuation. Then, despite my fears of childbirth, I wanted a family.

Cody James was born 11 months later, an adorable baby with soft curly blond locks that lulled me into thinking motherhood was easy. He definitely took after his father. Calm and easygoing from the beginning, he slept through the night from the second week. He cooed, hardly ever cried, and made me want another baby.

Crystal Rose was born 18 months later. The lusty cry she gave at birth should have warned me, but I mistakenly presumed she would be as angelic as her older brother. She wasn't. She was blessed with my strong-willed ways—and colicky besides.

I'll admit it, being the only child of a widowed man, I was spoiled and self-willed. Crystal definitely took after me, and within a month, though my nurse's training assured me differently, my weary body wondered if a person could die from lack of sleep.

Obviously, I did not die. Crystal is three now, and Cody is five. I feel blessed with a loving family.

I can't wait to get home. I never planned to work a double shift, but a friend needed me to fill in for her. That is what led up to my being in a dark alley close to midnight.

༺༻

I was only a few feet down the alley when I heard the hollow sound of something heavy connecting with someone's skull, followed by a man's groaning. My heart nearly leapt from my chest. Amazingly, I managed to swallow the cry that arose in my throat. I stopped, hardly daring to breathe, and listened.

Right then I should have turned and fled back out of the alley. I would love to try to convince myself that I didn't because I was brave and concerned for the poor soul ahead of me, but that wouldn't be honest of me. The truth is I was petrified and could not have fled if I had wanted to.

A deep voice not far from me snapped me out

A MURDER UNSEEN

of my state of shock.

"You didn't think we'd find out. Did you?"

I jumped, and how the man didn't hear me at that point I can't imagine. At first I thought he was talking to me, but then I heard the injured man respond in a raspy voice. "You won't get away with this. Someone will find out, someday."

"Maybe, but not today." The response was ominous.

I realized then that they were just on the other side of the dumpster to my right. I quietly stepped back into the protective shadow of the dumpster where the streetlight at the end of the alley would not expose me. All I wanted to do was to get out of there before my pounding heart alerted them to my presence. I clutched my purse tighter to my body, building up the courage to walk back the way I had come.

It was then that I heard the gunshot. The man was using a silencer, but it was definitely a gunshot. I heard the dead weight of a body slide down against the wall, falling to the ground with a thud. I felt shock. I felt bile rising in my throat. And I knew I was in trouble.

Easing back against the wall, wanting to make myself invisible, I waited for the inevitable footsteps. When I heard them, I let out a cautious sigh of relief. He was walking down the alley—away from me. I was lucky—luckier than the man on the other side of the dumpster.

A MURDER UNSEEN

I waited until his footsteps faded into oblivion and then turned to leave. The clattering sound of cans being knocked over sent my heart into spasms. I nearly laughed aloud when I realized that it was I who had knocked the cans over, and not the killer coming back to get me. I was on edge and wanted out of there as fast as I could. I hurried out of there with fear hovering like a black cloud over me.

No more shortcuts. I was headed to the safety of my car the long way.

As I reached the end of the alley, I caught a movement out of the corner of my eye. It was one of those moments in life when you don't think. You simply act. I swung my purse at the movement—and I wasn't carrying a lady's evening purse. My purse more closely resembled a small backpack and inside was everything from a wallet to a cell phone to a small pistol my father had insisted I always carry. Not that it was doing me much good in my purse. But then again, maybe it was. It was probably the pistol that slammed against my attacker's skull, knocking him out cold. At least I thought he was my attacker—and I thought he was out cold. I didn't stay around to find out. I was running before he hit the ground. I was running for the safety of my car. I was running for my life.

※※※※※※※※※

My hands were shaking as I pushed the clicker to unlock the car doors. I wanted the security of the locked vehicle. I wanted to put distance between the alley and myself. I wanted to call Henry and have him reassure me that all would be well.

Fastening my seat belt wasn't high on my priority list at that moment. The car was on and in drive in record time. I resisted the urge to burn rubber as I left the parking lot. If the murderer was watching, the last thing I wanted was to draw attention to myself, to have him suspect that I had witnessed the murder.

A witness? Could I really call myself a witness? I had seen nothing—but I knew a murder had taken place.

Once on the road I reached for my cell phone, pushing speed dial to reach Henry. I took deep breaths in a vain attempt to calm myself and slow the rapid beating of my heart as I waited for Henry to answer. It wasn't working very well.

"Hey, Babe, are you on your way home?" Henry's calm, reassuring voice reached out to me. His voice embodied everything that I wasn't at that moment.

"Henry...." That was all I could get out.

"Sandra, what's wrong?"

"I was going to take the shortcut through the alley," I began in a panic. "Henry, some—someone—oh—oh—my gosh, someone was murdered!"

Henry was careful in how he responded. He obviously sensed I was on the verge of breaking down completely—if I hadn't already reached that point.

"You saw a murder? You *witnessed* a murder?" he asked in a calm, measured voice.

"I...I didn't *see* a murder...so I guess you can't say I *witnessed* a murder...but I did hear a murder."

The words ran together.

"Are you sure?"

"Yes." I knew I sounded too emphatic, too defensive.

"Where are you right now?" His voice was reassuring.

"A few blocks from the hospital, close to the interstate. I probably should have returned to the hospital, but I didn't want a scene that would make people talk and draw attention to me."

"Turn around and head for the police station as you tell me what happened. I'm slipping my earpiece in so that I can get the kids into their car seats and meet you at the police station."

I knew I should object at Henry needing to get the kids up and dragging them off to a police station after midnight, but I couldn't. Henry was my solid rock. I wanted him with me. I wanted his comforting presence, his arm around me, his shoulder to lean on, and his calm directions in the midst of the turbulent storm that surrounded me at that moment. I needed Henry. I couldn't imagine life without him.

"Thank you."

"There's no way I'd let you go alone. Now tell

me what happened," he told me as I heard him rattling his car keys.

I took a deep breath and let it out slowly.

"Okay. I was only a few feet down the alley when I heard that hollow sound of something heavy connecting with someone's skull—and then I heard a man groaning. There was a dumpster between them and me. I froze in place. The next thing I heard was the injured man saying, 'You won't get away with this. Someone will find out, someday.'

"I don't know how they didn't hear me at that point. I nearly jumped out of my skin. I felt exposed and vulnerable, but somehow they didn't hear me. Then the shooter said, 'Maybe, but not today.'

"That's when I heard the gunshot—like from a gun with a silencer attached. I heard a body slide down against the wall, falling to the ground with a thud. I waited until the footsteps of the killer faded and then fled from the alley.

"As I reached the end of the alley, I caught a movement out of the corner of my eye. I was sure it was the killer. I was terrified and used the only weapon I had at hand."

"You used your gun?" Henry asked incredulously.

"No," I responded, embarrassed to a degree. "It was in my purse. I swung my purse at my attacker's skull and knocked him out cold. I didn't even wait to see how bad he may or may not have been hurt. I just ran."

A MURDER UNSEEN

Less than an hour after witnessing the murder, I was down at the police station, sitting in a dingy room at a wooden table that had seen better days. I felt like I was the guilty party being grilled.

Henry was at my side being supportive of my stance, yet somehow maintaining his cool at the lack of understanding and the disbelief on the part of the police officers. My cool had all but evaporated.

"You say you heard a man being shot?" It was an older gray-haired detective asking me the question. His doubts sounded through to his voice. I had learned earlier that his name was Darrel Fritz.

"Yes, that's what I told you," I answered for what seemed to be the hundredth time, though in reality I believe it was only the fifth.

"But you didn't see anything?" Detective Loren Trent countered.

"No, I didn't see anything. Like I told you, I was on the other side of the dumpster. I heard them talking."

"Tell me again what they said," Detective Darrel Fritz said, as if by my repeatedly telling them, my story would change. My fuse was getting short.

"Listen, I came here like any good citizen would to report a murder. You act as though I'm the one on trial!"

The third man, the one who was leaning up against the wall listening but never speaking, finally spoke up. His badge identified him as Detective Jordan Lewis.

"Mrs. Ford, the problem is we can't find a dead body in the alley."

"That can't be!—There at least has to be blood."

"Forensics says there is none."

I just stared at him, open mouthed, my mind trying to take this all in. Henry looked just as confused. I could see that he wanted to support me, but he wasn't sure how to argue this point. *I* wasn't sure how to argue this point!

"Listen, Lady, why don't you go home and get a good night's sleep. By your own admission, you worked two shifts back to back. You were probably just imagining things," Detective Lewis spoke down to me.

I didn't like that he was insinuating that I had imagined all this. His condescending attitude grated on me.

"Right, I imagined everything," I replied sarcastically. "And what about the man I knocked down with my purse. He was a figment of my imagination as well?"

He smiled—a definitely condescending smile. "I'm sure you hit something—but it wasn't a man. There was no one there."

Unless he was a drunk, I thought to myself, but I wasn't going to help their case out by saying it aloud.

Despite what it looked like to them, I knew what I had heard. I knew a man had died in that alley.

"You are sure the scene wasn't wiped clean?" Henry asked.

"We're sure," Detective Fritz assured us, his eyes sympathetic. He glanced over at Detective Lewis.

"I believe we are done here, Detective Lewis—unless you have any further questions?"

It was obvious that though Fritz disapproved of Lewis's methods, he agreed with his take on the situation.

The interview was over. I was too tired to argue. So they thought I was an overworked, hysterical female. Arguing with them wasn't going to help.

Detective Fritz ushered us out of the room like a grandfather reassuring his grandchildren that it was all a nightmare, nothing more. Henry was at my other side, his large hand wrapped protectively around my smaller hand. It didn't make sense. Maybe it would after a good night's sleep. Maybe things would be clearer in the morning.

We each picked up a sleeping child from the lobby couches, thanked the woman officer for watching over them, and headed for the car. We didn't speak until we were on the road again.

"Henry, could they be right?" I asked as we pulled out of the parking lot. "Did I imagine those things?"

"Did you hear what you heard?"

"Yes, I did...but could there be a less sinister explanation for what I heard?"

"I can't think of one," he replied. "One thing I know for sure. I believe you if you said you heard it. I would never doubt you. I trust you. And I love you."

"I love you too, Henry. Maybe after a good night's sleep it will all make more sense."

"It just might."

We were in bed shortly after arriving home. I thought I would be up half the night in worry, but exhaustion set in. I fell asleep with Henry's arms wrapped protectively around me.

Chapter 2

A Family Trip

"Mommy! Mommy! Wake up, Mommy!" Cody's voice penetrated through the deep fog of sleep that was wrapped around me.

"Mommy! Wake up!"

Another voice chimed in as Crystal scrambled up on the bed beside me, demanding my attention.

Opening my eyes, I tried to focus on the round, cherubic-like faces of my two children. Cody and Crystal were climbing on top of me, the excitement in their faces reminding me that I had forgotten what weekend this was. We were going camping.

"Okay, munchkins. Give your mom some room to breathe," Henry's deep voice caught my attention. He reached down, gently pushing a wayward strand of hair from my eyes.

"Listen, Sandra, you had a long night. *We* had a long night. If you want us to cancel our trip for today, I'll understand. I just wonder if it would be more therapeutic if we just got away."

I smiled up at him, my sensitive, caring husband, and knew that he was right. I didn't want to spend the weekend sitting at home fretting over what had or had not taken place last night. I needed a distraction for my conscious mind while I let my unconscious mind sift through the events.

"You're right as always," I replied as Crystal snuggled up against my side. I pulled my arms out from under the covers, wrapping them around her.

"When were you planning on leaving?" I asked.

"Half an hour ago," Henry responded with a laugh.

"What time is it?" I asked in surprise.

"Ten."

"Ten!" I exclaimed, pushing the covers off. "I'm sorry, honey. I must have missed the alarm. I didn't mean to sleep in."

"Slow down," Henry said with a grin. "I turned your alarm off. I figured you needed the sleep. I've packed the bags. All you need to do is get dressed."

A MURDER UNSEEN

I glanced back at the children, realizing for the first time that they were already dressed.

"Daddy made us pancakes," Cody announced, grinning up at me.

"I help him," Crystal announced in her baby voice.

"You sure did," Henry said as he ruffled her hair. "Daddy's got lots of big helpers, doesn't he?"

I smiled contentedly as I reached for clean clothes. Forget last night. I was so blessed.

I showered then—a cold shower to wake myself up. Feeling clean and awake, I looked in the mirror and wondered what Henry saw in me. With wet hair plastered against my head, my large brown eyes appeared sunken in my head. I looked like a drowned rat. *Lack of sleep. You don't always look this way*, I reminded myself as I reached for the hairdryer.

With my hair dried and styled, I studied myself critically in the mirror. Wavy brunette hair hung attractively over my shoulders, wisps of hair framing my somewhat angular face, softening it.

What women did before makeup was beyond me. I made the dark circles under my eyes disappear with concealer, followed by foundation. A touch of blush, some mascara and lipstick, and I decided I no longer looked like I had spent a double shift at the hospital and then witnessed a murder.

A MURDER UNSEEN

Soon we were speeding down the highway. Cody sat in front next to Henry, Crystal was strapped in her booster seat behind him, and I was curled up on the seat behind Henry. Just before I dropped off to sleep, I noticed the roads were becoming more winding as we entered the hills of Pennsylvania. New York was far behind us.

I'm not sure how long I had been asleep when I was startled awake by a loud bang and the feeling that our car had suddenly moved sharply to the right. Fear caused adrenalin to surge through my veins. The drop off to our right looked uncomfortably close as we careened wildly along the edge of the road, our car scrapping up against the guardrail.

I caught Henry's usually calm face in the mirror. He was anything but calm as he desperately tried to bring the car back onto the pavement. I could see the guardrail was going to end abruptly. Fear gripped me.

Crystal's cries made me turn to her, reaching out to somehow comfort her. Her usually sparkling eyes grew round and frightened as she stared out my window. I saw her mouth open in a scream. Jerking my head around to follow her line of vision, I saw a semi tractor-trailer encroaching upon us—ready to give us that fatal shove over the embankment.

The guardrail ended. My scream blended with that of my daughter's as our car plummeted over the embankment. I lost track of how many times the car rolled before coming to an abrupt stop, upside down.

A MURDER UNSEEN

At the force of the stop, my seat belt gave way, and I felt myself being thrown from the car through a space where my door used to be. The incline was steep. I felt the abuse my body was taking as I rolled further down the embankment.

Finally coming to a complete stop against some bushes, I rolled over, jerking my head up to scan the bank for the car. I was assaulted by searing pain as all the bruises and bangs I had been submitted to told me that quick movements were not recommended. The physical pain was nothing compared to the pain that tore my heart apart as my eyes focused on the unconscious bodies of my husband, and the two children I had borne him, dangling upside down in the demolished car.

I started up the embankment towards them, the physical pains of my body forgotten.

Breathe, please breathe! My mind screamed at the motionless bodies. *Move! Cry! Anything! Just prove to me that you are alive!*

But no one moved.

No one cried.

No one exhaled.

Nearing close enough to see the glazed over look of death in their eyes, my mind still defied what my eyes were seeing. It just could not be.

At that moment, the car burst into flames. I felt myself hitting the ground. I heard a blood curdling scream of denial, barely recognizing it as my own.

Instinctively, I lifted my arms to protect my face from the flying debris, but my eyes peered out from behind them. I wanted to tear my eyes away, but I was powerless to do so. I was mesmerized and in shock as I watched the flames destroy all I held dear. Tears rolled down my face, graciously obscuring my sight.

Nothing in my life had prepared me to handle this. I kept thinking to myself: *This can't be real. This can't be happening. I'll wake up any moment and realize this is all a horrible nightmare.*

But I didn't wake up.

It wasn't a nightmare.

It was reality.

Reality was enforced as my eyes caught a movement higher up on the embankment above the burning car. I saw the driver of the semi tractor-trailer, but he couldn't see me. I was hidden by the car.

My heart was pounding with fear as I watched as he peered down at the burning car. He didn't seem to realize that I had survived. My scream must have been absorbed by the explosion when the car burst into flames. If he discovered that I wasn't in the car, would he come after me?

No, this is all a mistake. A dreadful mistake! He's not trying to kill me. It was an accident!

But I didn't move. I was not convinced.

He was dialing a number on a cell phone. I flattened my body against the grass, hoping to be invisible as I strained to listen.

"Detective Lewis?"

A pause as he listened to someone on the other end.

"The loose end is tied up."

That's all he said, but it was enough. The murderer got back into the semi tractor-trailer and drove off.

Burying my face in the grass, I gave in to the great sobs of grief that racked my body. I knew I needed to leave, I knew I needed to run, but I couldn't bear to leave them. To leave them would make it final. I felt abandoned and alone.

If Detective Lewis was involved in this, who could I trust? I knew that I was in deep trouble and that I couldn't go to the police for help. I didn't have a clue what I was going to do.

One thing I did know: I wasn't going to tell anyone I was alive. Let them figure it out themselves. If they didn't, so much the better. If they did, hopefully by then I would be far, far away.

A MURDER UNSEEN

Chapter 3

The Cottage

It was late in the afternoon by the time I reached the other side of the gorge. Seeing a clearing up ahead, I stepped behind a large pine tree, peering around it through the trees. I could see what appeared to be a cottage nestled back against the woods at the far end of the clearing. I was hoping this was an empty cottage. I was numb and I was injured. I was in no shape to meet people.

I stood behind the trees at the edge of the clearing for some time, studying the cottage—if it really was a cottage. As I had drawn closer, I realized that the building was bigger than I had first imagined. It could be considered a lodge—someone's summer or winter retreat.

From where I stood, I had a clear view of the driveway. There was no car in sight, but that did not mean the place was vacant. I waited for twenty minutes as I listened and watched for any sign of life. There was none. I decided it was time to check the place out.

Walking through the woods to the side of the building, I was pleased to find the edge of the woods ran closer up to the building at that point. Cautiously, I approached the lodge and stood under a window. I listened. There was no noise.

I eased my way along the side of the house until I was near the back door and listened again. Nothing. I tried the doorknob, but it was locked. I walked quietly around to the front door. It too was locked.

By now I was convinced that no one was home. I began to test each window, not bothering to be quiet anymore, and eventually was rewarded for my efforts. A side window was unlocked. Pushing it open, I hoisted my sore aching body up to the windowsill and practically fell into the room on the other side in a crumpled heap.

Moaning from the added abuse to my already abused body, I didn't even try to get up. I curled up in the fetal position and buried my face in my arms. I was alone. I did not need to be on guard. I didn't try to understand. I didn't try to rationalize. I didn't even try to think. I simply gave in to the tears.

A MURDER UNSEEN

I lost track of time. I only knew that it had been dark for some time when I actually sat up and wiped the tears from my face. I didn't want to get up. I didn't want to think about what I needed to do next. The only thing I wanted to do was hit rewind on the recording of my life and get back to before the murder. Why had I taken the shortcut?

I got up anyway. I stood up slowly, feeling the stiffness that had settled into my joints. Stumbling along the wall in the dark, I reached the door and switched on the light.

I found myself in a bedroom. It was decidedly not the bedroom of a single man. A woman's touch was evident in the quilt covering the sleigh-style bed, in the lace tablecloth adorning the round bedside table, and the silk flowers in the cream-colored vase. An antique dresser was against the wall opposite the bed.

If a woman's touch was evident in the room, I reasoned that woman's clothes should be in the drawers. I walked over and opened the top drawer only to find it empty. I opened drawer after drawer, but it was useless. There were no clothes to be found—and I needed new clothing if I was to remain inconspicuous. My shirt was torn at the sleeve, and though my jeans weren't torn, they were streaked and stained from my fall.

It was then that I saw the closet off to the left, near the door. Opening the closet doors I let out a sigh of relief. There wasn't much inside, but I didn't need much. There was nothing fancy, but I didn't need anything fancy. What was inside was weekend wear, but it looked durable and comfortable. Pulling a black cotton t-shirt from the hanger, I held it up against me. It was a bit big, but it would do. Rummaging through what remained in the closet, I chose a plaid flannel shirt. It would do as a light jacket, which I would probably need before this was over. There were no jeans or slacks, but from the looks of the shirts, the jeans probably wouldn't have fit me anyway. I would have to wash mine.

A hall closet held an automatic washer and dryer. I was in luck. Above them on the shelf were detergent, clean linens and towels. Grabbing a towel from the shelf, I threw in a small load of wash before heading for the bathroom to shower.

I turned the shower on as hot as I could take it. I was reminded of my cold shower earlier that morning. How could life have changed so quickly? Tears mingled with the water as it ran down my face. I asked myself once again if this could be real? Emotionally I was raw.

Being raised as an only child, I have already admitted that my father spoiled me. It also meant I was raised by a man, a very logical man that would not put up with me acting irrationally. He was always telling me, "Think with your mind—not your emotions."

I used to hate it when he would say that. But

those words came to mind now, and despite the fact that I knew I had all the right in the world to give in to my emotions, I knew if I was to survive I needed to think with my mind. Somehow I had to put my emotions on hold and think with my mind.

But not tonight. The tears continued to mingle with the hot water as it ran over my tired and bruised body.

A MURDER UNSEEN

Chapter 4

The Plan

    The next morning I knew it was time to come up with a plan. It was a necessity for survival.
    I was planning on running, though I hadn't figured out how or where. The thought had come to me during the early morning hours that, if I was going to run, shouldn't I first access what was left of my inheritance?
    The inheritance from my father was safely set aside in a bank back in our hometown. It was saved for retirement. Should I dare try to access it? If I used my ATM card it would take me quite a while to access it all since there are limits on how much can be withdrawn each day. And time was my enemy.

A MURDER UNSEEN

If they presumed me dead, my accounts would be frozen, but if I was able to get home and personally go into the bank today, there was a good chance my accounts would not yet be frozen.

I could empty the account. I knew there was in the vicinity of $30,000 in the account. Thirty thousand plus interest.

Of course, by doing this I would be proving that I was definitely alive and well. But, I reasoned, they would surely figure that out when they found but three dead bodies in the car. It was only a matter of time before they knew.

If I was to be on the run, I would prefer to be on the run with money. Retirement did not seem something wise to save for under the circumstances. I could be dead by tomorrow if I weren't careful.

My mind was made up. I would grab my money and run for it. I would begin a new life, in a new place, under a new alias—just like in the movies. But how come in the movies it sounded so glamorous? In real life my heart felt raw and my stomach would not stop cramping.

Reaching for my purse, I wondered how long it would take me to walk to the nearest town. It was then that the thought came to me: The garage!

Fumbling with the door connecting the breezeway to the garage, I found it was locked, which only made me more determined than ever to get in there. If they locked it, they must have something valuable in there—like a car!

A key? Where would they keep a spare key? Where would *I* keep a spare key?

The kitchen drawers? I rummaged through them. There were no keys in there. I ran my fingers along the ledge above the doorframe, and sure enough, there was a key. I put it in the lock and turned it. The door opened.

There was no car, but there was a Harley Davidson 350. It wasn't what I had been hoping for, but it would sure beat walking out of there.

※※※※※※※※※

The bike ran like a charm. Soon I was entering my old town by a side street. Part of me yearned to go by my house, to see it, to return to it as though none of this had transpired. I could not risk it.

The bank was worth the risk—but not the house. I had to leave the past behind and I knew I would not be able to if I saw my house and all the reminders it held of a loving husband and two wonderful children.

I parked on a side street behind the bank where questions would not be raised over my new mode of transport. At least no one would miss the bike until next weekend—if they even went to the cottage then. On that one count, I had time on my side.

Walking into the bank, I was greeted by Janice West, a long-time friend. I felt myself wavering. Could I go through with this? Maybe I ought to just go to the police after all.

No! That was the logical side of my brain screaming. *Look what happened the last time you went to the police!*

I smiled amicably as Janice greeted me. "How can I help you today, Sandra?"

"I was hoping I would be able to speak with the manager. It is concerning my personal savings account."

"That could be arranged. Why don't you take a seat for a minute while I see how soon the manager will be available."

I sat down and waited. It really was only a few minutes, but it felt like an eternity. Each time the door opened I expected to see Detective Jordan Lewis entering. How he could hurt me in public without raising suspicions against himself I did not know, but I knew he could find a way. Somehow he was connected with the murder in the alley. For some reason he was covering it up and he wanted me out of the way—permanently.

I heard a voice call my name. I could see the manager now.

"I would like to close out my savings account," I told him after the initial pleasantries.

"You want to close your savings account?" the manager replied in a half question.

"Yes. Is there a problem with that?" I asked as though this were a natural request. I could think of at least a dozen problems.

"No," he replied slowly. "It's just a highly unusual request in light of your previous business patterns with us. May I ask if everything is okay?"

"Everything is fine," I lied, amazed that my voice remained steady. "It's a personal matter and I appreciate your cooperation and utmost privacy in this matter."

"But of course," he responded. "Let me see," he said as he glanced over at the account register on the computer screen. "You realize this could take some time?"

I had considered that—and I knew time was something that I did not have. I couldn't get too greedy right now. I would have to take what I could get and run.

"I wondered if that would be the case. If I could have $20,000 right now, I can wait for the remainder," I responded, hoping my request was reasonable. I wasn't convinced it was. I had never requested such a large sum at one time before.

"We can manage $20,000," he replied. He rang the intercom for his secretary.

Twenty minutes later, I walked out of the bank with $20,000 in my purse. I could feel eyes on my back. I knew that despite how I had praised the banker on the confidentiality of his institution, that within several hours the whole town would know and their tongues would be wagging. Then they would hear of my family's death and their tongues would wag again. What story would they construe to explain my actions? I really didn't care. I was past caring. I just wanted to run and hide.

Chapter 5

The Journey

Driving to a nearby town, I pushed the motorcycle into the river at the outside of town and watched it sink to the bottom. No one would find it for a long time. I walked into town and went on a shopping spree at the local Wal-Mart.

I was going to live in jeans, t-shirts, and sneakers for the next while. I also bought a box of hair dye, and the result was that now, instead of being a brunette, my hair was black. I dyed it in a public restroom along the lakefront, a natural place to leave with wet hair. I cut it short and dyed it. Henry always loved my long wavy hair and couldn't bear the thought of my cutting it short. But Henry

A MURDER UNSEEN

was no longer around to admire it. And if he were, he would be the first to tell me to cut it under the present circumstances. At least that is what I told myself as I chopped it off, carefully stuffed it all in the plastic Wal-Mart bag along with the used up box of hair color, and tossed it in the trash bin outside. He would understand my need to look like someone else. This was the quickest change.

I headed for the bus station and watched the latest newscast as I waited for my bus to arrive. It all seemed so surreal. My picture was being shown on all major broadcasts—but not the way I always dreamed I would make the news.

The police had changed their story. No longer were they denying that a man had been killed in the alley. They were now saying that I killed the man and then attacked an innocent bystander who had seen me do it. They believed it was a drug-related killing. Not that I was using drugs, but selling them. I could have laughed out loud at their ridiculous attempt to frame me, except that I knew it was working. I could see it in the eyes of those around me.

My actions were the added proof they needed. After killing the man had I not fled? The deaths of my precious family were under investigation as well. They were alluding to the fact that I was responsible. Had I not fled with $20,000? I'm sure they had come up with some way to explain that it was dirty money and not a legitimate inheritance.

No one took a second look at me as I watched the report, a disgusted look fixed on my face, the look of someone who couldn't believe a person could be so vile. I wondered how many others before me had been framed in much the same manner.

The bus arrived and I headed south. I needed time. I needed somewhere to go where doing nothing could be considered the norm. That would only work if I headed to the nation's vacation capital. Thus, I was on my way to Florida.

I stayed in Florida for several weeks. For the first few days I pretty much barricaded myself in my motel room. There I gave in to an overwhelming grief, a grief so strong that I feared I would be consumed by it. I let the tears flow. I cried in anguish at my great loss. I cried in fear of my uncertain future. I cried out with an irrational anger at my family for leaving me alone in the world, and a rage I would not have believed possible welled in my heart towards those responsible for my family's death. My emotions were raw and unpredictable.

After several days, I began to leave my motel room just enough to not draw unneeded attention. I took long walks on the beaches in the early mornings and late afternoons. When in the public eye I tried to act as though I didn't have a care in the world. I practiced living a lie. I practiced being someone I was not.

Back in my motel room, I would give in once more to the grief. I needed this time. I wasn't ready to face the future. I needed time to mourn.

I also knew that although twenty thousand sounds like a lot of money, that it would not last forever. I would need a nest egg set aside for when they caught up with me and I needed to run again. It was inevitable. To deny it was dangerous.

I can't say I was done mourning. I don't think you ever quit mourning. But the time came when I knew it was time to move on. I had decided by this time that Florida was not the best place to stay. With water on three sides I felt like my options for escape were limited. I wanted more options—and I wanted to be yet farther from New York. California was to be my next stop.

Chapter 6

California

California is a better place to hide than Florida—though the beaches in Florida are definitely more to my liking. I will always choose warm waves over the frigid ones of California beaches. I'm just not tough enough to turn into a California beach bum.
    I spent the summer as a part-time employee at a local restaurant while living in a rundown apartment in a not-so-great part of town. One summer was enough for me. I was exhausted from living in fear that the next person who entered the restaurant would either recognize me—or be there to kill me.

A MURDER UNSEEN

I applied for a position as a maid. They accepted me on face value because they knew the owner of the restaurant where I worked for the summer. He vouched for me.

It turned out better than I expected. Though they advertised for a maid, they were really hoping for a live-in maid/nanny. It turns out that Ed and Sally Jones have three children: a four-year-old daughter, Kendra; and eighteen-month-old identical twin boys, Cory and Colt.

Surprisingly, I find myself in a new home and working for a family that seems as genuinely sweet as they come.

I have a studio apartment to myself above the garage. It is small, but adequate. It is tastefully decorated in muted rose and blue. I fell in love with the apartment the moment I saw it.

My days begin early—but no earlier than the hours I kept as a nurse. I rise at six, get dressed, and fix my own breakfast before heading over to the main house.

It turns out that Ed is a doctor—just like Henry was. I wonder if the hurt will ever end. The ache goes so deep. It is still so raw. I thought it would get easier. Sometimes I'll think it has. Then something happens—like finding out that Ed is a doctor—and the harsh reality of what happened to my family returns. The feelings in those moments are as real and raw as they were when I watched in horror as my family's lives were extinguished.

It's hard to believe that Henry and my babies are really gone. I still find myself rolling over to snuggle up to Henry in the dark hours of the night—to find nothing but a cold empty bed to my side. I've lost count of the nights I have soaked my bed with tears.

One cool night, the windows were open. I heard one of the twin's cry reach out to me through the still night air. I awakened, momentarily transported back in time, and got up to get Crystal from her bed. The realization that it was not her hit me like a ton of bricks, the realization that she'll never cry out for me again. I sat huddled in the corner of my room, shaking and overcome with grief.

But mornings always come. I wash my face and I force a cheerful smile to lighten my countenance. I have become the consummate actor.

Thankfully, the children distract me during the day—in a good way. I look after the children from seven until noon while Sally hides herself in the study. She is writing her fourth book.

At first, I tried to keep Sally at an arm's length, but there are some people you just can't help but grow fond of. Sally is one of those people. We take time for coffee together in the mornings around ten, and she joins us for lunch.

I didn't know if I would survive those first months, caring for another's children, being reminded constantly of what I had lost. But as time went on, despite grief-stricken nights, in the end I found it was therapeutic. I ended up throwing my love into those children and letting them begin the healing process in my life. A healing process that I now realize will never be complete. The hurt will never go away, but somehow I must learn to live with it and to move on.

After lunch, Sally looks after the children while I clean the house. She makes dinner. I must admit she is a much better cook than I am. She insists I eat dinner with them. At first I resisted, but I have grown to appreciate them. They have accepted me as part of their family. I need that connection—despite the fact that I will never tell them the truth of my past. If anyone comes close to revealing the truth, I will run before I will allow them to be endangered.

Chapter 7

Roger

It was nearing the end of my first month at my new job. The ringing of the doorbell went unnoticed as I ran the vacuum over the living room rug. I was settled into my daily routine by now. It was one of those odd days when Sally had taken the children to the mall with her—so the house was empty but for me and the vacuum.

Suddenly I felt someone tapping me on the shoulder. Not one to startle easily, I thought nothing of it as I flipped the vacuum off and turned to greet Sally and the kids.

That's when I reacted.

A gasp of shock escaped my lips as I found

myself looking up into a ruggedly handsome face that should not have been in the house.

My eyes quickly spied the gun in a shoulder holster—and the badge hanging from the hip. It was the sight of the badge—and not the shock of finding a strange man in the house—that made my face blanch. *How had the police found me?*

"I'm sorry," he apologized before I had time to formulate a response in my mind, a response that probably would have resulted in my getting locked up.

"You're Pamela, right?"

"Yes," I managed to get the words out as my heart pounded unreasonably in my chest. He had called me by my alias, Pamela—and that was significant. He didn't *act* like he was here to arrest me.

He motioned toward the door as if that explained it all. It didn't and he caught that.

"I rang the doorbell—but no one answered. So I let myself in," he explained—as if that made any sense to me.

"I'm Roger, Sally's brother. Is she home?"

I let out an embarrassed laugh of relief as it all began to make sense.

"Sally went to the mall with the children. She said she would be back around four."

"Do you mind if I wait here?" he asked. It was really only a polite question. I knew Sally well enough to know her home would always be open to her brother. I just wished she had told me she *had* a brother—and that he was a police detective! My heart was still racing, although I now realized he was not here to handcuff me and take me in.

"There's a fresh pot of coffee in the kitchen if you'd like to help yourself to some. I put it on just before I started vacuuming in here," I rattled on, relief loosening my tongue.

"You'll be done soon?"

"Yes, I just need to put the vacuum away."

"Well then, why don't I pour two cups and you can join me," he said, a twinkle in his eyes. "It's the least I can do after scaring you like that. I thought you were going to pass out on me."

I smiled what I hoped looked like a genuine smile.

"Sure, I'll join you in a minute," I told him even though it was the last thing I wanted to do—but I could see no polite way out of it. I definitely did not want to give him cause to wonder about me.

※※※※※※※※※

"Sally has nothing but praises to sing about you," he told me as I stirred the sugar into my coffee.

"You have a great sister to work for."

"So you enjoy your work?" he asked.

"Yes, I guess I really do," I replied, immediately wishing I had left the doubt out of my voice.

"You didn't think you would?"

"I wasn't sure. I've worked with children before,"—I didn't bother to add that they had been my own—"but had never had any experience with twins." I hoped I was digging my way out and not further in.

"They are an experience all of their own, that's for sure."

"Definitely, but I'm learning how to keep up with them." I smiled.

"Where did you work before?" he asked the inevitable question.

"I worked at a restaurant over by the beach for the summer, but I guess I just wasn't cut out for that."

"You don't sound like you're from here, though I'll admit that I can't place your accent."

"That's because I'm a Heinz 57 mixture. My dad was military," I explained. "It seemed like we moved constantly. I guess I picked up a bit of every type of accent."

This was all the truth. My father had been in the military and we had moved at least once a year. From day one with the Joneses, I had decided that I would tell my true life story up to a point—up to the point where I began my nurses' training. I couldn't afford to admit I was a nurse. I couldn't afford to admit that I had been married to a doctor. I couldn't afford to admit that I had had two children, a son and a daughter. I couldn't afford to fit the profile of the accused murderer that I had become.

He nodded his head in understanding. My answer seemed to satisfy him. I relaxed.

"Where's your dad now?"

"He died of a heart attack when I was 18," I said, suddenly focused on my coffee. I didn't want to get into the subject.

"I'm sorry," Roger spoke quietly.

"So am I. ... But life goes on. You just keep going. That's one thing I have learned the hard way," I said, forcing a half smile onto my face as I looked up at him.

"You're right. Life can hand us some pretty tough ones. I find what holds me up and together through the good and the bad times is my relationship with God. I don't know how I even tried to handle life without Him before. I sure tried for a long time—but I was miserable.

"Knowing He is in control and that He loved me enough to send His Son to die on the cross to pay my penalty for sin—wow!—that's plain amazing.

"And He loves me enough to give me the strength and grace to not just get through each day, but to live each day to its fullest with Him."

I think it was at that moment that he realized I didn't have a clue what he was talking about. I definitely didn't. I had never heard someone speak so passionately, yet naturally, about spiritual things.

I had been preached at before by pious people who spoke down to me as they reeked of pride and hypocritical lives. Consequently, I never really heard what they said. I guess this all showed in my eyes and Roger saw it.

"You don't know what I'm talking about, do you?"

"Not really."

It wasn't the greatest of responses—and one that I feared would lead to a conversation I wasn't ready to have. Though it was obvious that this was something very real to Roger, and I felt a strange feeling of envy at the obvious peace he had in his life, I was not ready for any claims God may have wanted to put on my life.

It was a great relief to me that the house erupted with noise at that moment. Sally walked in with the children. Kendra was holding a large red helium balloon. She was chattering away a mile a minute. I hoped my sigh of relief was not too noticeable.

Cory and Colt toddled over to their Uncle Roger with squeals of delight. He reached down, pulling one twin up on each of his knees that were suddenly transformed into horses from the Wild West.

"Roger! It is so good to see you! When did you get back to town? I thought you weren't getting home until next week?" Sally exclaimed, a pleased smile lighting her face.

"I'm back early, and of course I had to come see my favorite sister—and my niece and nephews."

"His favorite and *only* sister," Sally said to

me, then turning her attention back to her brother, whom she obviously adored, she asked, "When did you get here?"

"About half an hour ago. I about scared the life out of Pamela!" Roger laughed at the recollection.

"I was vacuuming and didn't hear him come in," I defended myself sheepishly.

Sally laughed. "Well, I had better get some supper on," she said as she reached for the meat in the freezer.

"Can I give you a hand?" I volunteered, not ready for any more personal questions.

"Sure. I would appreciate that."

※※※※※※※※※※

That evening, after the children were in bed, Sally insisted I join them in the living room for coffee and cookies.

"Sally told me how you two met this afternoon," Ed chuckled.

"It was a bit of a surprise meeting," I admitted.

"Did he spend the rest of the afternoon boring you with what he does for a living?"

"Actually, he didn't," I replied.

"Now, Ed, his stories can't be any worse than the medical stories I have to put up with from you! Your stories have more blood and guts in them than

A MURDER UNSEEN

Roger's by a long shot!" Sally defended her brother.

"That's how doctors are, Sally," I agreed without thinking it through.

"And what would you know about doctors and their stories? I haven't told you hardly any, at least not yet!" Ed retorted good-naturedly.

"I dated a doctor once," I answered quickly—too quickly. I wished I could have pulled it back.

"Obviously you didn't like him or his stories enough to stick it out with him," Ed teased.

Somehow, I managed to swallow the lump in my throat and even managed a joking response, but I felt like I had been kicked in the gut.

The spirit of the evening was lost.

All I could think of was Henry and my children. My Henry. The man with whom I really did want to stick it out. We had vowed to stay together 'till death do us part—and I still couldn't believe that death had truly separated us. I was also reminded that I would never be able to truly relax with people again—and that realization hurt.

I turned to Roger in an attempt to pull the attention away from myself.

"What do you actually do?" I asked him.

"I work in narcotics."

"That must be interesting work," I heard myself calmly saying as my stomach churned. *Why on earth did he have to work in narcotics?* This conversation was going from bad to worse.

"I never would have described it that way, but

I guess it is," Roger replied as I wondered if my wanted poster had made it this far west. I wondered if he had seen it. I wondered if the conversation would make it connect in his mind if he had.

It didn't. The evening ended without my being arrested.

I went to bed that night and cried bitterly for the life I had lost, for a past that I could not recover, and for the lives of my husband and children.

༺༻༺༻༺༻༺༻༺༻

But that was nearing the end of my first month with the Joneses. Time has passed. Kendra celebrated her fifth birthday last week. The twins are in the terrible twos stage with all the challenges that presents—but they are so cute and adorable that it's hard to stay frustrated with them.

Time has ironed out many of the difficulties. Obviously my wanted poster hasn't come to Roger's attention and the family accepts me just as I am. Of course, they still don't know the truth about my past, but they trust me—and I love my new life with them.

And Roger? That's another story in and of itself. Somehow I have been able to overcome my fear of his profession and have accepted him as the big brother I never had. He has helped me in more ways than he realizes.

It became apparent very quickly that talking about God, and his relationship with God, came as easy as breathing to Roger.

Time also proved that whatever it was he had with this God of his was real. It showed in his life. I hold great respect for Roger.

The fact that I'm not ready to accept Roger's religion for myself has never affected Roger's acceptance of me as a person or as a friend. Maybe that is the most significant part for me. I know he cares about me unconditionally. Maybe that means his God could really love me too. Maybe.... But, I still have my doubts. I'm living a lie. I can't see God accepting that.

Despite our differences, Roger has helped me begin to heal—at least as much as one can expect healing. Maybe it's because I know he really does care.

By the way he looks at me at times, I know he wonders about my past, but he doesn't press for answers. I also know he cares for me on a deeper level than either of us is ready to admit.

Not that I'm not attracted to him. What woman wouldn't be? Of course, it took me a long time to admit to myself that I could be attracted to him, that I could possibly love someone other than Henry. At first, it felt paramount to adultery to even consider that I had feelings for Roger. And I knew it wouldn't work. Roger is a police officer; I am a fugitive from the law. Roger has his God; I respect his religion, but it isn't for me. It would never work—but it was a comforting thought.

There have been times I have wanted to tell him everything. It would be a relief in many ways. But it remains a fact that he is an officer of the law and he would be responsible to turn me in if he knew the truth. Since I'm not convinced that even an excellent lawyer could clear my name, I'm not ready to take that chance. I am no closer to knowing how to remedy my problem than I was that first night, but I have accepted my lot in life.

A MURDER UNSEEN

Chapter 8

Discovered

Jostling my purchases around so I could catch a glimpse of my watch, I realized I was running late. I would have to hurry to catch the bus, but it had been a profitable day at the mall. I felt good about my purchases. Among other things, I had finally found the perfect sweater, a black button up with a V-neck. Simple, but perfect.

Finding my way impeded by the crowds of weekend shoppers, I knew I was going to miss the bus. The idea came to me to take a shortcut through the basement garage. It would be quieter down there and I would be able to move faster. There would be no crowds and no congestion. I hurried for the

A MURDER UNSEEN

elevator, managing to be the last person to squeeze in.

By the time the elevator reached the basement level where the parking was located, I was the only one aboard. Walking briskly across the nearly deserted parking lot toward the elevator at the far end of the building, my solitary footsteps rang out loud and clear. I smiled smugly. I wasn't going to miss my bus after all.

I saw a woman and child in the distance as they walked out of the elevator. I was almost there. I smiled at them when they passed me. The little girl was chattering away, her eyes sparkling with life. She was probably about seven. They were definitely mother and daughter. They had the same eyes, the same slightly upturned nose, and the same full lips.

I reached the elevator and pushed the up button. Out of habit, I looked at my watch again. I smiled. I had time to spare. Watching the lighted numbers over the door, I followed the elevator's descent. Two more floors and it would be here.

Suddenly the quietness of the nearly empty parking lot was broken by the sound of a rapidly approaching vehicle. I turned to glance at the oncoming vehicle. It was a Toyota, red and flashy.

Teenagers, I thought as I took a step closer to the elevator.

Shaking my head, wishing they would catch the disapproving look in my eyes, I peered through the windshield of the oncoming truck. What I saw made my heart turn cold with fear and paralyzed my body.

Though I could not clearly see their faces yet, it was obvious that they were not teenagers, but two men. They were two men with a mission.

There was no doubt that I was connected to this mission. The semiautomatic rifle pointing out the passenger side window left no doubts of their intent in my mind. They were waiting for the truck to draw just that much closer, waiting for that perfect shot.

Immobility did an abrupt turnaround to frantic mobility as adrenaline kicked in. Desperately, I pushed the up button again and again as I watched in hopeless terror. They were racing closer, their faces becoming distinguishable.

It was then that I recognized one. It was the face that haunted me in my nightmares, the face of the man who had called Detective Jordan after forcing our car off the road. It was the man responsible for my family's death!

And now he was going to finish the job.

And there was nowhere to run.

Open! My mind silently screamed the word as I pounded frantically on the elevator doors. My only hope lay in the elevator doors miraculously opening.

Turning, I saw the gun being leveled at me. There was a sadistically triumphant gleam in the man's dark eyes. I thought my heart had stopped already—and then my miracle happened. The elevator doors slid open and I practically fell in.

A bullet grazed my upper arm as I dropped to the floor. I heard myself screaming and knew it was more from fear of the ricocheting bullet within the confines of the elevator than from the pain itself.

I heard brakes being slammed and the truck door opening. They were coming after me!

Desperately, I pulled myself upright and pushed the close button and the button to every floor in the building. The doors closed as the pounding of feet drew near. I collapsed against the wall of the elevator, shaking. My purchases lay sprawled on the floor before me. They weren't important now.

The elevator jerked upwards as I pressed heavily against its cold metal interior. I was panting, shaking, and feeling like I was going to be sick. *How had they found me?*

At the next floor, the elevator jolted to a stop and the doors opened. Two teenage girls stood there giggling. They took one step in—and then saw me and stepped back out. Their giggling ceased. Their eyes grew wide. Screams came from their lips.

I must have been a frightful sight at that moment, sprawled as I was against the wall, my shirtsleeve soaked with blood, my face stark white in comparison. I was in shock.

There was no time to feel sorry for them. Their cries had alerted a security officer. Seeing him hurrying in my direction, my numbed brain finally began to kick in. The ramifications of being questioned by the police shocked me into action. I had to get away! I couldn't risk such a high profile position with the police.

I pushed the close button as the security officer focused on my face, the concern on his face instantly turning to suspicion as the doors closed, blocking him out.

I pushed the buttons for the third and fourth floors as my brain raced. I would get off on the third floor.

Emptying my bags, I quickly wrapped one of my new T-shirts around the wound. Doing so all but stopped the blood flow. I threw my new sweater over my shoulders, effectively hiding the all-too-visible bloodstained shirt.

The elevator jolted to a stop. I was out as soon as the doors were open. I walked briskly—but not too briskly—toward the restrooms around the corner. I was going to be sick and I knew it. I was going to be sick from the pain, but also from fear. My stomach churned.

I was barely in the toilet stall when the heaving began. At least the restroom was empty. When the heaving subsided, I sat on the edge of the toilet with my head between my knees, hoping I wouldn't pass out. I needed some blood flowing to my brain. I needed to be able to think.

I also needed a plan and I needed it quickly. Sally was going to get worried any minute when I didn't show up in time for supper. I needed to call with an excuse, because I really had to go back to my apartment. I wasn't in any shape to hide out on the streets. I needed a chance to heal if I was going to run. If....

I didn't want to run. I was enjoying my new life and knew it would be hard to start all over again. Next time I may not be so lucky. I definitely didn't want to run—but could I find a way out of this?

At that moment, I couldn't think of a way out. Of course, I was having a hard time thinking at all. I had to buy myself time. A plan formulated in my mind.

Slowly, I raised my head. I was still lightheaded, but I didn't pass out. Very slowly, I stood up, smiling with nervous relief when I realized my plan might work. I had a phone call to make.

"Joneses' residence," Sally answered.

"Sally?"

"Pamela, is that you?"

"Yes, it's me. Sorry, but I'm running late."

"I was starting to get worried. I was about ready to send the National Guard after you," Sally teased.

"Oh, you know how it gets when I'm shopping."

"Of course I do. Do you want me to send Roger down to pick you up. He's here for supper tonight."

Roger was there. That was not what I needed!

"No, don't bother," I answered calmly as the

knot in my stomach grew tighter.

"I'll save some supper for you to heat up when you get back."

"Please don't bother. I think I'm coming down with the flu or something."

"Then for sure I'm going to send Roger over to pick you up," Sally insisted.

"No. No, don't do that. It's not necessary. I have a few more errands and then I'll head home. I'm fine. Really," I lied through my teeth as my arm ached furiously at my side. "I'll see you in the morning."

"If you insist," Sally replied hesitantly.

"But thanks a bunch, Sally."

"See you tomorrow then."

"Okay. Good night."

I hung up the phone and let out a deep breath of relief—if there could be anything near relief in the dire circumstances I found myself.

For better or for worse, my plan was underway. Sally had been called and would not be expecting me at the house that evening. A few more miracles—like getting out of the mall *unnoticed*, buying medical supplies at the Long's Drugs on the corner *unnoticed*, and getting on the bus *unnoticed* by my assailants—and maybe I would get safely home.

A MURDER UNSEEN

Getting out of the mall unnoticed was surprisingly easy. Buying supplies at the Long's Drugs on the corner didn't even result in a casual comment from the sales clerk. But walking to the bus stop and hoping not to be noticed by my assailants—that taxed my nerves greatly.

I kept expecting my would-be murderers to materialize before me. I wondered if they would keep coming after me and how efficient they would be at tracking me down. I wondered how they had found me. I wondered if they knew where I lived. I wondered how well the security guard had seen my face. I wondered if he would be able to identify me. I wondered a lot of things.

My would-be murderers did not materialize before me and soon I was climbing off the bus a few blocks from home.

Shifting my bags, one knocked against my arm. A red-hot pain shot down to my fingertips. Biting back the cry that rose in my throat, I walked on. Somehow, I made it those few blocks.

Drawing near to the house, I saw a dark figure step out from the shadow of the doorway. My heart felt like it stopped and was then frantically trying to climb out of my throat.

What an idiot I am! If they found me at the mall, they must know where I live! I've walked right into their trap!

The thoughts flashed through my mind in an instant. I was just about to act, to drop my packages, and to dive behind the hedge bordering the front of the house when I saw my assailant's face.

It was Roger.

It was just Roger.

My body shook from the release of the tension and fear. In that strange moment, I suddenly began remembering things I should have remembered back at the mall. My picture in the newspaper. My picture as I was bent over doing CPR on the body of an elderly lady that had passed out right in front of me at the mall.

I had acted without considering the consequences. I saved her life—and got my picture pasted on a prominent page of the local paper.

Luckily, I'd had the presence of mind to disappear before the reporters could question me. They never discovered my name. Therefore, it stood to reason that they would not necessarily know where I lived. Somehow, I had convinced the Joneses not to tell anyone, to let me remain the "anonymous heroine."

Obviously, my enemies had seen the picture. They had recognized me. They had staked out the mall. And tonight they had almost killed me.

As Roger approached, I took the time to adjust my packages, trying to buy enough time to pull myself together, to steady my trembling hands. I was shaking like a leaf.

I wished it were Sally instead of Roger waiting to meet me. I knew I could fool her.

A MURDER UNSEEN

But Roger? He is trained to be observant. It is part of his job—and not a trait that disappears just because he's off duty.

If he were anything but an officer of the law, maybe I could tell him. Maybe he would believe me and keep my secret and we would carry on as though it had never happened.

The fact of the matter is that Roger is not a salesman. Roger is not a business owner. Roger is an officer of the law. As such, he would be obligated to turn me in—and I'm not convinced I would be able to clear my name. It would be my word against theirs. My actions, and the fact that I fled, would condemn me in the eyes of the jury.

Roger was walking down the driveway to meet me now. I pasted a smile on my face. I hoped I could fool him.

"Let me give you a hand with your bags," Roger said, a grin tugging at the corner of his lips. "What did you do? Buy out the store?"

"No, I did not!" I retorted playfully, shuffling the bags around once more, making sure he did not take the bag with my few extra purchases of medical supplies. I did not need any questions concerning my sudden interest in stocking my medicine cabinet, especially since by tomorrow Roger was bound to know of the shooting at the mall.

I began to doubt my sanity in returning, but I had to. I needed a few days to recuperate before I ran again.

My heart ached. An empty, hopeless feeling was coming over me. I did not want to run again.

At my apartment, I thanked Roger for his help as he placed my bags on the bench by the door.

"You really aren't feeling well, are you?" he said as he studied my face in the light for the first time.

I wondered how bad I looked. The concern in his eyes reminded me that I would miss him dreadfully when I ran. He was a true friend.

"No, I don't feel good. Hopefully, it's only a 24-hour bug."

"I hope so," Roger sympathized. "Well, you had better get some sleep. I'll talk to you soon. Get better."

"Thanks for carrying my things up for me," I called after him as he walked out.

As soon as he was gone, I locked the door and began fumbling with my sweater. Underneath, drying blood and fresh blood mingled together, effectively holding my shirt to my arm like glue. I desperately hoped it wasn't half as bad as it looked.

Carrying the bag with my newly purchased medical supplies with my good arm, I headed for the bathroom. Easing myself to a sitting position by the bathtub, I meticulously laid my medical supplies on the floor in front of me. Everything in order. That was the nurse in me.

Turning to kneel beside the tub, I held my arm under the faucet, allowing the warm water to loosen my shirt. It was a slow process, but eventually I was able to remove it.

I gently moved my arm to get a better view of the wound and gave myself a halfhearted smile as I realized the wound wasn't near as bad as it felt—a strange consolation.

Knowing from a strictly clinical point of view that I was not going to die did little to ease the throbbing in my arm. It did nothing to change the feeling that I was about to pass out right there on the bathroom floor. I gave myself a pep talk that would have made my nursing instructor proud.

Reaching for a tube of triple antibiotic, I emptied the tube, filling in the jagged red crease in my arm. It was bleeding again. I felt weak and lightheaded, but somehow managed to apply the gauze and wrap up my arm.

With my arm finally wrapped, and the bleeding all but stopped, I reached for the painkillers. Fumbling with the lid on the acetaminophen, I managed to get it open and dumped three pills into my shaking hands.

Slowly pulling myself to a standing position, I waited for a wave of nausea to pass before stumbling over to the bathroom sink. I poured a small glass of water and downed the pills.

Ignoring the pain as best I could, I grabbed a towel. I used the wall for support and worked my way out of the bathroom and over to the bed. I pulled back the sheets with my good arm and eased myself back against the pillow with the towel under my arm—just in case it started bleeding again. With my arm throbbing, I wasn't sure if I would be able to sleep. Those were my last thoughts as I drifted off into a sleep brought on by pure exhaustion.

A MURDER UNSEEN

Chapter 9

Secrets

Beep. Beep. Beep. The insistent sound of the alarm clock cut through the physical exhaustion of my unconscious mind, forcing me to an unwanted conscious state. Automatically I reached for it, and was immediately reminded of the night before as stabbing pain raced back and forth along my arm. I forgot about the alarm momentarily as I cradled my arm against my body, waiting for the pain to subside.

When the throbbing came down to a bearable level, I swung my good arm around to hit the alarm off, then lay back against the pillow. I was wide awake now and wondering how I was supposed to keep this incident a secret. *How could I hide the fact that I had been shot? How could I function in my present condition?*

Since they would not expect me down at the house for at least an hour, I had time to think. It took all but a few minutes to decide I didn't really need to think. What I needed was a day or two in bed. I needed a few days to recuperate, to make sure the bleeding was not going to start all over again.

I made the agonizing trip over to the phone.

"Hello." I heard Sally's voice over the line.

"Sally, this is Pamela."

"How are you feeling this morning?"

"Not so great. I'm running a fever and just feel raunchy. I think it would be better if I stayed in bed for the day."

"I'll bring some breakfast up to you in a little bit," Sally volunteered.

"No, don't bother. I have a few things up here, and anyway, I really don't feel like eating right now."

"Are you sure?"

"Positive," I told her firmly.

"Well, if you need anything, give me a call. Okay?"

"I promise," I assured her before hanging up.

I spent the rest of the day near the bed, nursing my arm, drinking lots of fluids, and downing as many painkillers as was safe. Sally called a few times, wanting to bring me something to eat. I politely turned down every offer, reassuring her that

I had everything I needed. And I did. Everything but a good doctor for my arm, along with a whiz bang of a lawyer who had a detective under his employ that could find out what had really transpired in the alley with no real facts to go on.

I shook my head sadly at my predicament and fought back the urge to cry. My father had not raised me to be a crybaby. I had always tried to be the tough kid who rolled with the punches. Of course, the punches in life were getting worse and crying was beginning to be a way of life.

I had lots of time to think, so think I did. I had never thought much about God before meeting Roger. I hadn't been convinced He existed. At the same time, I couldn't go along with the big bang theory—even if the majority of the great minds of the world believed it. It just didn't make sense to me—especially after nursing school. Our bodies are so complex, so intricately designed. I just couldn't believe we just happened by chance.

The question remained: How do you explain the alternative to happenstance? Of that, I was not sure. I pretty much decided to just ignore the possibilities. If I agreed that these intricately designed bodies of ours needed a Designer or Creator, then would not that make me accountable to Him? I was not ready to go that far.

I guess that meant I was not an atheist. I guess I leaned toward believing there had to be someone who created this world we live in, someone who was in control, someone who was in charge of life and death. But to go as far as to say that this Creator, this in-charge-someone, actually had a say in my life? I wasn't ready to agree with that.

What came after death? I wasn't sure and didn't really want to think about that—so I didn't. Not even when my family died. I refused to consider the possibilities.

That was as far as my idea of God went. I figured He must exist, but I wasn't going to let that fact impact my life. At least that is how I had always viewed it. The problem is that now I was face-to-face with my own mortality for the second time. Questions about life after death were at the forefront of my mind.

I couldn't understand Roger's theory of a personal God who is interested in our welfare, who wanted a personal relationship with us. That was going too far in my mind. I wanted to keep God at a distance. He could be that "big man in the sky," but He was not to get personal.

I was ready to admit that Roger's relationship with God did seem real, but it wasn't for me. I still figured God wouldn't want someone like me, a fugitive from the law. Sure I was innocent of what they accused me of—but I was running. I was living a lie. I didn't really want God. I didn't want to be accountable. I didn't want to be held responsible for my actions. I just wanted to live my life—at least what was left of it.

When the phone rang close to suppertime, I knew it had to be Sally again, and instinctively knew that this time I wouldn't be able to put her off. When she offered to bring up some toast and ginger ale, I relented.

Before she came, I changed into sweat pants and a baggy sweatshirt. I had changed the bandage earlier and had been pleased to find the bleeding had stopped. I applied the new bandage much thinner, keeping it invisible under the sweatshirt.

I met her at the door.

"You really don't look so great," Sally told me as she set out the food on the table.

"Thanks," I grimaced back at her.

"I mean...," Sally stammered.

I laughed.

"That's just what you meant—but no offense taken."

"I guess I've never seen you sick before. Are you feeling any better tonight?"

"A little," I admitted, which was the truth. I remained standing, hoping she would catch the hint and leave me to eat alone. "I'm thinking I'll need another day. Can I give you a call in the morning?"

"Of course," Sally responded. "I'll leave you to eat."

"Thanks so much, Sally," I called after her as she headed out the door.

The next day went about the same, except that Roger called. He wondered how I was doing. I assured him I would be up and around the next day.

※※※※※※※※※

True to my prediction, I was up and around the following day. I was a bit slow on my feet and still running a low grade fever, but apparently my body was fighting off the infection on its own. I went about my daily routine, using my left arm as little as possible.

Roger showed up for supper. I'm convinced he really came to check on me. It was sweet of him, but it scared me that he might realize that all was not as it seemed.

"You're up and around," he stated the obvious as he plopped his hat down on the side table.

"As predicted," I responded.

"You still look a bit under the weather."

"Between you and Sally I'm going to get a complex," I protested with a laugh. "I can't look *that* bad!"

I poured him a cup of coffee as he laughed at my comment.

"Sally!" I called out over my shoulder. "Roger is early. Do you want to join us for a cup of coffee?"

Sally came out smiling with a hug for her brother.

"Did you hear of the shooting over at the mall?" Roger asked after a few minutes of light conversation.

"What shooting?" I asked innocently, studying the intent in his eyes. It didn't seem to be an interrogation, but an honest question. I relaxed inwardly.

"You didn't hear?" Sally responded in surprise. "It was all over the news the other day."

"No. What happened?" I asked again.

"It was at the Paramount Mall," Roger began. "A security guard was alerted to a problem when he rushed to the elevator where two teenage girls had started to scream. Before the doors closed, he saw a woman inside bleeding. She had obviously been shot. His suspicions were aroused when he realized that she had intentionally closed the doors. Witnesses came forward saying they had heard gunshots in the basement."

"And then she just disappeared," Sally added.

"Why would she just disappear?" I asked in feigned surprise.

"My presumption would be that she is running scared." That was Roger's opinion.

"Do you think the gunmen found her?" The fear in my eyes was real. It was my own personal nightmare—that they would find me!

"That's one theory. If they haven't, I would bet my life on it that they are looking for her."

"Why? You don't think it was a random shooting?" Sally asked in concern.

"No, if that had been the case she would more

than likely have headed straight for the security guard—not run from him."

He stopped to sip some coffee, cradling the mug in his hands. "I think she knew who her would-be killers were."

I thought about that one as I sat there. Life would get complicated if Roger found out I was that woman and I wasn't able to convince him that I didn't know them.

One step at a time, I reminded myself as I sipped my coffee. *One step at a time.*

❦❦❦❦❦❦❦❦❦❦

The next step came sooner than I expected.

After supper, Sally and I were clearing the table while the men visited in the living room. I thought I was doing so well, carrying things, not letting on that my left arm still experienced shooting pain with every movement—and then Sally bumped into me.

She could not have hit my wound more directly if she had planned it all out in advance. The corner of the cake pan slammed right into my arm, and I didn't have time to consider my reaction. I just reacted, dropping the plates from my hands.

My cry of pain mingled with the sounds of shattering dishes on the floor. I grabbed my arm, albeit gently, while Sally stood by, apologizing profusely. I caught sight of Roger and Ed heading in from the living room, and that brought me to my senses.

"The dishes! How could I be so clumsy! I'm so sorry, Sally," I apologized profusely as I bent down to pick up the larger broken pieces—and working hard at ignoring Roger's questioning look.

"No, it's my fault. I ran right into you," Sally responded. "Let me have a look at your arm. How is it?"

I glanced down at it as though it were nothing.

"It's fine," I lied as pain raced the length of my arm, ending in a fiery, tingly sensation in my fingertips. "I guess the corner of the pan hit a nerve. You know, like your funny bone." I tried to brush it off.

Thankfully, Sally bought my act and went for the broom. She started sweeping up the smaller pieces. I was thankful she took the initiative because I knew I wasn't capable of sweeping right then. My arm felt like it was on fire and my biggest fear was that it would start bleeding again, right there with people to notice it.

Thankfully, it didn't.

With the table cleared and the dishes in the dishwasher, Sally and I joined the men in the living room for coffee. I can't really remember what we talked about the rest of the evening, but I thought I did a pretty good job of hiding my pain. I was quieter than usual, but then everyone was that night.

"I think I'll turn in early," I said during a lull in the conversation.

Roger stood up beside me.

"I'll walk you up," he said in a normal voice, but something in his eyes made me feel unsettled. But what was I to say?

We walked in silence across the driveway to the stairway up to my apartment. As we neared the bottom of the stairs, he broke the uneasy silence.

"Do you want to talk about it?"

"About what?" I asked, turning startled eyes on him. I felt like a trapped animal. He knew—or at least suspected something.

He didn't respond immediately, but looked me squarely in the eyes for a long minute. I hardly dared to blink. By a conscious effort, I didn't fidget with my hands, I didn't tighten my jaw, I didn't swallow hard or move my lips. I didn't want to look guilty.

"About the shooting."

"About the shooting?" I feigned confusion, keeping a perplexed look fixed on my face while my stomach churned. This was getting bad.

"What do you mean?" I asked.

"You know what I mean."

"No, I don't," I responded a bit too defensively.

"Let me see your arm."

"What does my arm have to do with this?" I responded too quickly.

"Let me see your arm," Roger repeated, this time more firmly.

"Roger," I protested, "I don't know what your problem is tonight, but I'm tired. I'll see you in the morning. Good night."

I turned to walk away from him, but he reached out, grasping my wounded arm in a gentle yet firm manner. I gasped in pain. And right then I knew I was in trouble.

"Pamela, I'm sorry. I didn't want to do that."

I knew he didn't. I could hardly believe he had done it. But he had. And now he knew. I was still holding my arm, my face contorted with pain, but I turned to look at him.

"Let me walk you up to your room. We'll talk there."

I nodded in agreement and let him usher me up the stairs. I didn't see that I had a choice.

Once we were in the apartment, he sat me down in one of the chairs while he rummaged through the medicine cabinet for painkillers.

"How many do you want?"

"Give me three."

"How bad is it?"

"It's not that bad," I replied as I popped the pills with my good arm, washing them down with a glass of water. Seeing the skeptical look in his eyes, I added, "The bullet grazed my arm. It left a mean looking crease, but it's fine. It just hurts."

"Let me see it," he said as he reached to help me take off my sweater and then rolled up my short sleeves. I watched as he gently pulled back the gauze.

"Ouch. That must have hurt."

He taped fresh gauze in place before talking again.

"Tell me what happened." It wasn't a request. It was a demand.

I began my story, trying to keep detached. I knew I was on the verge of tears and I didn't want to cry.

"I was running late. The mall was packed full so I decided to take the elevator to the basement and cut across to the other side down there. It worked great. It was nearly empty and I made good time.

"But then, when I was waiting for the elevator, a truck came toward me, too quickly for a basement garage. At first I thought it was a bunch of rowdy teens, but when I saw the gun sticking out the passenger window I knew I was in trouble. There were two people in the truck, but I didn't get a good look at them. It all happened so fast."

"What happened next?"

"I was in a panic. I kept hitting the up button and hoping the elevator would arrive. I wanted the doors to open so I could escape. There was nowhere else to run. Then the doors opened, and I fell in as the gun was fired."

"That's when you were hit?"

I nodded my head and then closed my eyes tightly, trying to cut out the slow motion movie my mind was playing for me. But the images remained.

I opened my eyes, staring off into space. I continued my story, but it was impossible to keep detached anymore. My voice cracked.

"I pushed the button for the next few floors. At the next floor, the doors opened. Two teenage girls were about to board—and then they saw me. They screamed." My lower lip quivered as I remembered my fear and terror reflected in their faces. I bit my lower lip, struggling to stop it from trembling before continuing.

"I pushed the door close button.—I don't know why. The look on their faces?" I shook my head. "I guess I just couldn't stand seeing my own fear mirrored in their eyes. So I threw on a sweater, covering the blood, before getting off at the next floor."

"Why didn't you find a security guard instead of coming home on the bus? Why didn't you tell *me* when I met you outside?"

I could see hurt in his eyes. I could hear it in his voice. Hurt and anger mingled together. I hadn't trusted him.

Shaking my head, I answered slowly, hesitantly, searching for the best way out of a very sticky situation. "I...I don't know. I...I panicked. I was scared and not thinking clearly."

I felt a twitch at the corner of my lips, one of those nervous twitches I can't avoid when I'm emotionally stressed. Roger saw it and reached for my hand.

"You weren't thinking at all. But listen, you are going to be all right. We will find these men. Do you think you could identify them?"

"No, I doubt that," I answered too quickly as distinct images of their faces flashed before my eyes.

"You had to have been able to see them," Roger insisted.

"It all happened so fast. I just didn't get a good look," I protested.

"Do you remember passing a mother and daughter?"

"Yes, now that you say that, I do."

"The mother got the license plate number and we are looking for them now. *When* we find them, I want you to come and pick them out of a lineup."

"I...I can't do that," I insisted.

"Can't or won't?" Roger countered quietly, catching me off guard.

"I...I," I stammered too slowly, too uncertainly. He was watching me and he knew the truth. He knew I could identify the gunmen.

"I want you to come down to the station tomorrow and answer some questions. For the record," was all he said next.

"All right," I replied weakly.

"I'll be there with you. It will be fine," Roger told me in a reassuring voice. "I'll pick you up around ten."

"What about Ed and Sally?"

"Do you want to tell them, or would you

prefer if I did?"

"Could you?" I asked quietly.

"Sure. I'll tell them." He stood to leave. "I'll bring Ed up here after I've talked to them to look at your arm. He could prescribe some stronger painkillers. You could use them."

It wasn't a question.

"Thank you," was the best response I could I come up with.

And then he was gone. Morning would come soon enough.

A MURDER UNSEEN

Chapter 10

Questioned

"You never saw those men before?" Detective Graham asked again as I finished my story.

"I already told you that I didn't get a good look at them." I was tired of his line of questioning. I was tired of the whole ordeal and fearful of the outcome.

"If you didn't see them, I guess it would be hard to know. My problem is that I'm just not convinced you didn't get a good look at them."

I glared at him. I was angry now.

"*I'm* the one who was shot at. *I'm* the one who agreed to come in here and tell you what happened. *I'm* the victim in this situation. Why don't you quit treating me like I'm the criminal and go find those men!"

I stood to leave. "I don't think I have to put up with this."

"Pamela," Roger's voice was quiet, but full of authority. "Calm down and sit down."

I just looked at him as though he were from another world. He was supposed to be on my side.

"Why?" I finally stammered.

"He's trying to help you," he stated calmly.

"He," I pointed emphatically at the detective across the table, "is trying to help me?"

"Yes." Roger was unruffled by my outburst.

I shook my head, but I sat down.

"We stand a much better chance of finding them if you can describe them for us. I know you saw them," Roger said calmly. "You pretty much told me so last night. Admit it, Pamela. We want to help you, but we need your help."

I dropped my head and tried to think. The painkillers I had taken in the morning were wearing off. My arm was beginning to throb again and I was having trouble thinking clearly. Worse than that, I was having trouble thinking rationally—and I knew that was dangerous.

"Okay," I sighed deeply as I lifted my head. "I saw them. I didn't get the best look at them, but I could probably identify them."

Half-truths would have to do.

Half-truths were safer.

Half-truths were at least more believable.

"But I didn't know them, and I'm really scared and confused and wish I could hit rewind and end this nightmare."

"Fair enough," Detective Graham replied. "Now we're getting somewhere."

"Can I go home now?" I asked wearily.

"After you've given us a description and looked through some mug shots."

It wasn't the answer I wanted, but it was better than what the outcome could have been. I gave them a description, keeping it intentionally vague, but close enough to their real description that, if they were caught, it could not be said I had lied. Thankfully, none of the mug shots matched.

It was early afternoon by the time we were finished and Roger gave me a ride home. There was an uneasy silence between us.

A MURDER UNSEEN

Chapter 11

Discovered

It was mid-afternoon. The sky was clear, the sun bright and hot. I was on the back porch heading to my apartment when I heard Roger's voice.

"Where's Pamela?" There was a tense urgency to his voice that I didn't like. I froze where I was and listened.

"She went up to her room. She should be back any minute.—Roger, what's the matter?" Sally demanded.

"I need to take her in for more questioning," Roger answered sharply, in marked contrast to his normal tone. My heart nearly missed a beat.

What did he know? How much did he know?

A MURDER UNSEEN

"Why?—What's wrong?" Sally stammered. "Please, Roger. Tell me what's happening. I think I have a right to know."

Roger let out a deep breath. "Her name isn't Pamela Hunter."

My mouth went dry. My heart pounded so hard it seemed to be vibrating in my skull. If he knew that much....

I didn't wait around to hear more. Any minute he would come looking for me. I stepped off the porch, keeping close to the wall of the house. Working my way behind the garage, I peered down the driveway. As I feared, another officer stood by a car in front.

I slipped out the back gate into the alley beyond and sprinted to the end of the alley. From there I slowed to a jog in order not to attract undue attention to myself. I jogged until my lungs felt ready to burst and my legs ached. My arm throbbed in protest. My only thought for the moment was to get as much distance as possible from the police—as much distance as possible from Roger. Suddenly those two are synonymous.

As I left the housing area, entering the business section of town, my mind started searching for a place to hide. My mind—not my eyes.

I knew I had to come up with somewhere safe, somewhere no one would look—somewhere that I could hole up in for a few days while my arm healed and the immediate frenzy of looking for me wore off.

A MURDER UNSEEN

I had enough money stashed away to make a run for it and start over again—but it would be difficult right now to walk unnoticed into the bus station and retrieve it from the locker there.

They would be looking for me.

Both sides would be looking for me.

And then it came to me. About a mile away was an old apartment building that had been condemned and boarded up. It had been on the news. Thankfully, it wasn't going to be demolished for several more months. That was where I headed. No one would be there. It was the perfect hideout.

That the police would come after me, I had no doubt. By running, I was as good as admitting my guilt. They believed I was guilty of using someone else's identification. That was mild in comparison to what they would find out if I stayed. That I was innocent of murder wouldn't matter. I couldn't prove it.

Nearing the condemned building, I walked casually to the back of it. With a quick glance around to make sure no one was watching, I walked briskly up against the building to check out the windows and doorways for one that wasn't boarded up. My persistence finally paid off. One window on the first level was boarded, but with only one board.

I took another quick glance around to reassure myself that no one was in sight. Pressing my foot up against the wall for support, I pulled on the board with all the strength I could muster with my one good arm.

It gave way and I tumbled over backwards on the grass, landing on my bad arm. I smothered a cry of pain with difficulty, and then lay gasping, waiting for the initial wave of pain to subside.

With my arm still throbbing, but the shooting pain gone, I sat up. Picking up the board, I knocked out the rest of the already broken window and then climbed through. By now, all I wanted to do was sit down and cry, but I needed to find a room to make my temporary home.

It didn't take as long as I thought. I found a room at the back of the building that was clean—at least clean in comparison to the others.

Inspecting each of the windows, I chose the one with fewer boards nailed on. I pushed on them, loosening them, but not knocking them all the way off. There was my alternative escape route.

I sat down on the dusty floor and closed my eyes. I was exhausted from the physical duress of the past days. Emotionally and psychologically I was hanging on by a thread. I tried to block out the pain, the loneliness, and the hopelessness that was threatening to overwhelm me.

Somewhere along the line, I must have fallen asleep. When I awoke, my neck had an awful kink in it and my stomach told me I had missed supper. It was growing dusk.

The building was cold and eerie in the dim light. I closed my eyes again, trying to ignore the growling of my stomach and the ache in my arm.

Sleep was slow in coming the second time round. I didn't want to admit it, but I was scared. I wanted to think I was tough and could handle life, but I knew I wasn't.

For the first time, I wasn't sure which way to turn. My options were so narrow, so confining. I considered turning myself in, which in many ways seemed like the easiest option. I was sure I would lose in a court of law—or be killed beforehand. But it would be over. There would be no more running.

The biggest drawback I saw would be facing Roger, Sally, and the family. How could I explain the double life I had been living? How could I explain all the lies? How could I live with their believing the lies and accusations?

I knew I couldn't tell them the truth. I couldn't risk their lives. I had already lost one family and I wasn't ready to lose my newly adopted family—as that was what they were to me.

No, I reasoned, it would be better to run. If I were caught, let it be far from here.

I stared into the darkness that now surrounded me and felt it seeping into my soul. How had I come to this point? I used to enjoy life. I loved my life with Henry and our children. Amazingly, I had learned to love again with my adopted family. And now this….

I did fall asleep somewhere in the midst of my thoughts—and then the nightmares came. I was transported back in time. I was in our car again being pushed over the edge of the road. My daughter's mouth was open in a scream. Her face was so real. In my dream, I reached out to touch her face—and then she was gone!

I awoke with a start to a dark, cold room. I awoke to blackness. I shook uncontrollably and started to cry.

By the time the first rays of dawn filtered through the boards covering the windows, I was out of tears. My heart was broken. I lay in an emotional stupor. I just couldn't imagine how it was going to work out this time. Capture seemed imminent. I didn't have the energy to run. Where would I go this time?

I lay in a fog for hours. It wasn't until early afternoon that my mind was capable of conceiving a plan. I began mulling over one plan after another, throwing each out as unrealistic. And on and on it went.

By late afternoon, I decided I wasn't going to give up. I wouldn't turn myself in. That would defeat all I had managed to accomplish in the past. I also knew I couldn't just start over again and wait for the next time I was tripped up. I had to prove my innocence. That was the only way to really move on with my life. Tomorrow I would start my trek back to where it all began. I would head back to New York and begin investigating.

Chapter 12

No Place to Hide

It was a slight sound that awakened me, so slight that when I opened my eyes I still wasn't sure why. I listened attentively for a full minute, not daring to move, before I heard another sound. It was the soft sound of footsteps in the hall outside my room. I held my breath, daring to hope the intruder would pass by. He didn't. The footsteps stopped outside my room. I saw the doorknob turning.

I leapt to my feet and had two boards knocked off the barricaded window before a strong hand restrained me. I swung around, kicking my opponent in the shins, but he didn't let go.

And then I heard his voice.

"Pamela, stop it."

It was Roger. The same deep voice, though strangely impersonal. I fought all the harder, refusing to answer, refusing to look at him.

He shoved me up against the wall with my good arm bent up behind me. My face was pressed against the rough wall of the condemned building. I had that strange feeling of oneness with the building. We were both condemned. I felt Roger snapping handcuffs on my wrists. I struggled against him, even knowing it was useless.

"Don't make this any worse than it already is," Roger's voice was strained and strangely apologetic.

"It can't get any worse," I answered defiantly through gritted teeth. There could be no apologies. I had to distance myself from him emotionally—and him from me. It was the only way to protect him. It was the only way to protect his family that I had come to love.

"Why?" he demanded as he swung me around, holding me roughly up against the wall. "Are you saying you *did* kill her?" His eyes were narrow slits, serious and searching my eyes.

My face dropped in shock. *Her?* The gender was not lost on me. This was *someone* different. This was *something* different than I had been anticipating.

"Did you kill her?" he demanded again, his eyes hard.

"What?" I exclaimed in disbelief. "Kill who?"

The defiance was gone. I was in shock—and

Roger saw it. He was studying me quizzically now. He wasn't sure what to think. Of course, neither did I.

"If you didn't kill her, why did you run?"

"Kill who?" I asked again.

"Pamela Hunter."

"Pamela Hunter? ... What happened to the real Pamela Hunter?" I asked in fear, a tremble to my voice. I really didn't want to know.

"Pamela Hunter was found dead in a motel room. She was shot at close range. The murder weapon was never found. Her purse was there, but her wallet was missing."

"And you think I murdered her?" I asked the question slowly, in disbelief.

"You tell me. I don't know what to think anymore," Roger responded, his grip still firm.

"I did not kill her," I replied slowly, my eyes locked on his. "I never met her. I found her wallet in a waste basket in a public restroom. You've got to believe me." I was pleading now.

"Why?" Roger answered me, his eyes hardened by betrayal. His voice was angry. "Why should I believe you? I thought I knew you. And suddenly I find out I don't even know your real name. I find out you're living under someone else's identity. Someone who was murdered. An unsolved murder. And you ran. You heard me talking to Sally, didn't you?"

I nodded my head. I didn't trust my voice. I

had never seen Roger angry before.

"If you didn't kill her, why did you run?"

"I...I can't tell you," I managed to get the words out even as my lower lip quivered. At the look in his eyes, I lowered mine. Things were definitely getting worse.

"Then I can't help you," Roger responded sharply as he firmly propelled me toward the door.

I didn't fight. I didn't have any fight left in me. As I walked out the doorway into the hall, I caught sight of someone a few doors down. At first I thought it was Roger's partner—but then I saw his face. That face. The face that haunted me in the dark of the night. The face that promised that one day it would get me. More than that, there was a gun in his hand.

I froze.

Suddenly Roger was shoving me down as a bullet whistled above us. With my hands cuffed behind me, I hit the floor hard. Roger's body impacted hard against mine—and then he was shooting at the fleeing man. It ended as suddenly as it began.

"Are you okay?" Roger asked as he rolled me over.

My response was a cry of pain as my injured arm brushed against the hard floor. Roger pulled me to a sitting position up against the wall. My breathing was heavy. Roger was kneeling beside me wiping the blood off my lip with the corner of his shirt. I wondered how badly my face was bruised and cut.

He asked me again, more gently this time, "Are you okay?"

My response was sarcasm. "I'm fine. I'm doing great. Best day I've had in a long time."

Roger ignored the sarcasm in my voice. "It's the same man." He stated it as though it was a fact, but I could tell he wanted my confirmation.

I opened my eyes. Roger was looking at me. The hardness in his eyes was gone, replaced by a confused wariness.

I lowered my eyes, swallowed hard, and then looked back at Roger. "You're right. It's the same man."

"Why is he trying to kill you?"

I opened my mouth to speak, but images of Henry, Cody, and Crystal swirled before my eyes. My mind went cold. What would they do to Roger and his family if they thought they knew? I couldn't be responsible for the deaths of any more people. I just couldn't.

"Pamela, tell me," Roger insisted firmly.

I looked back at Roger and I could see my face mirrored in his eyes. I was as white as a sheet. My eyes were filled with terror. Roger saw my terror and knew I wasn't going to tell him anything. I couldn't.

I shook my head, not in defiance, but wearily, almost sadly. "I can't tell you, Roger." I closed my eyes as if that would make it all go away.

"I can't help you if you don't tell me what's going on."

"I don't want your help," I lied to him as I tried not to cry.

"Open your eyes and tell me to my face that you don't want my help, and maybe I'll believe you."

I didn't want to. I didn't know if I could pull it off. But I did. I opened my eyes. They were moist, but determined. "I don't want your help," I told him steadily. "Just turn me in, forget you ever knew me, and let things fall as they fall."

"I can't do that."

"Do it for Sally's sake. For Kendra and the twins' sakes."

Roger studied me thoughtfully for what felt like an eternity. It was probably less than a minute.

"What type of trouble are you in?"

"Roger, drop it," I told him through gritted teeth.

"I told you, I can't."

I let my head drop as I fought back the tears. Then Roger's hand was under my chin, lifting my head up. My lips were trembling, my eyes tightly closed, but the tears were escaping anyway.

"I asked you a question: What type of trouble are you in?" he asked again, patiently.

I shook my head.

"Nothing will happen to Sally or the kids. I promise you."

I opened my eyes at that.

"Don't make promises you can't keep. You don't know what you're talking about," I answered him harshly in my pain.

"Then explain it for me."

I shook my head. "I...can't," I answered him in a trembling voice.

He just looked at me, frustration etched on his face. Then he shook his head.

"I guess you haven't left me any other alternative. Let's go," he said as he helped me to my feet. There was a heaviness in his voice, a resignation to the fact that he could not help me.

A MURDER UNSEEN

Chapter 13

My Name Is...

My stomach tightened into a hard knot as Roger led me into the police station. I wasn't ready for this—but then, who would ever be ready for this?

I felt my natural bent toward sarcasm rising to the surface. I had already dished some out to Roger. It was my defense against breaking down and crying—and I needed a big line of defense right now.

Everything was unreal. It was ludicrous. It should never have happened in the first place. I should never have taken the shortcut through the back alley. I should never have heard the man being killed. My family should never have been killed. And I shouldn't be here right now.

A MURDER UNSEEN

"Your name?" a brusque voice asked.

I jerked my head up as his voice brought me back to reality.

"My name?" I responded dumbly while my brain did tailspins. To tell or not to tell? Was there any use hiding the truth any longer? Wouldn't they find out soon enough? Was it worth fighting?

"Your name," the officer spoke again and there was no pleasantness to his voice.

I swallowed hard.

"Sandra.—Sandra Ford." I answered the rest of the questions mechanically.

I was numb. I watched as they tossed my personal effects into a tray—my watch and some loose change from my pocket. And then they asked for my ring. The ring. My last material connection to Henry. It was a gold ring with a pearl set beside an onyx. Henry had given it to me on our first Valentine's Day together. I can see and hear him even now in my mind's eye, kneeling in front of me, the blue velvet box unopened in his extended hand.

"You are my princess, and I am your knight in shining armor," he had told me, his eyes sparkling. I had opened the box and there we were: the pearl and the onyx.

Where are you now? I wanted to shout out. *I need a knight in shining armor! I need someone to tell the world I didn't kill you!*

But he wasn't there. He was dead.

The ring was dropped unfeelingly into the

tray. I swallowed hard at the loss, but I refused to cry.

Everything seemed surreal as they fingerprinted me and took my mug shot. *This can't really be happening,* I kept thinking to myself. But it was. Somehow I maintained my composure through it all.

※※※※※※※※※

"You have been advised of your rights?" Detective Graham asked as he sat down across the table from me.

"Yes, I have."

"You were using Pamela Hunter's ID." It was a statement, not a question.

I nodded my head.

"Why did you kill Pamela Hunter?"

"I didn't kill her."

"Then how did you get her wallet?" It wasn't a pleasant question.

"I found it in a trash can in a restroom."

"When? What was the date?" He was jotting down something in his little black book.

"I don't remember the exact date, but it would have been last June."

"Where was this restroom?"

"At a bus station in Tampa, Florida."

He was comparing what I was telling him against his notes. Obviously it rang true as to the location at least.

"Your real name is Sandra Ford?" He changed the direction of his questioning.

"Yes," I admitted. It sounded strange to hear my name again. It didn't even sound like my name anymore.

"Why did you need a new identity?"

"Why I needed a new identity, and the fact that Pamela Hunter is dead, have nothing to do with each another," I answered, sidestepping the question. "I didn't kill Pamela Hunter. I never even met her."

"I still need to know why you needed to take on a new identity," Detective Graham persisted.

I wondered if he already knew. I thought not. I felt Roger's eyes on me, and I didn't want to answer the question.

"Could I speak to her alone?" Roger asked.

I wasn't sure if I should feel pleased or terrified at the prospect, but figured I really didn't have a lot to say in the matter.

Detective Graham looked at him thoughtfully for a moment. "All right."

The door was barely shut when Roger started speaking. "Off the record, did you kill her?" he asked, his eyes searching my face for the truth, searching for any telltale signs of deception.

I heard the concern and caring in his voice—and I couldn't understand it. I had deceived him from the time we had met, and yet, somehow, he still cared about what happened to me.

"The police seem to believe I did. Isn't that

good enough for you?" I answered coldly, hoping to alienate myself from him.

"That's not what I asked. I asked you if you killed her."

He was waiting. I could feel his eyes penetrating me. I closed my eyes and swallowed hard.

"Did you kill her? A simple yes or no is all that I'm asking for," Roger persisted.

I looked across the table at him and shook my head. "It doesn't matter. They'll prove I did."

"You didn't do it," he said then. It wasn't a question. It was a statement. He believed me. I know that should have been a comforting thought, but at that moment I was still worried.

"No," I sighed. "I didn't kill her."

"Tell me what happened."

"You don't want to know. Really," I protested weakly.

"Yes, I do," Roger insisted.

"Why? Why do you care?" I asked in bewilderment. "I've lived a lie before you since the day you met me. Why should you care what happens to me? You don't really even know me."

"Pamela, I do know you. I know who and what you've been since the day I met you. And one thing I know is that you are not a murderer," he told me confidently, using the name he knew me as—as if to make a point.

"It could get you killed," I told him bluntly,

my chin in the air, quivering, defying him to argue on that point.

"I'm willing to take that chance."

"What about Sally and the kids? Are you willing to risk their lives?" I asked quietly now, the defiance gone, my eyes locked on him.

"You can't keep running," he responded slowly.

I nodded my head, blinking back a tear.

A knock on the door saved me—or so I thought. Roger walked to the door, opening it.

"Here's the report you wanted," I heard a young officer say.

I turned in time to see the door close behind Detective Graham as he re-entered the room. Roger was reading the report. His eyes narrowed. His jaw tensed. The knock on the door wasn't going to save me. It had just condemned me.

Roger was lifting his head up. I quickly averted my gaze, but not before catching a glimpse of the shocked expression on Roger's face. I was suddenly very interested in studying my shoe laces. I wasn't ready to face him. I wasn't sure if I'd ever be ready to face him.

"What does it say?" Detective Graham asked. Roger's reaction hadn't been lost on him. Neither had mine.

I could feel Roger's eyes on me. I could hear the stunned disbelief in his voice. "Sandra Ford is wanted for the murder of an FBI agent back in 2008.

She was known to be at the scene of the crime." Roger's voice cracked. It was barely noticeable, but I heard it. I could tell this was hard for him to swallow. He didn't want to believe it—which was a bit of a consolation to me—but there it was in a written report. He was still talking.

"Her husband and two young children were killed in an automobile accident the following day that they believe she engineered. She disappeared after emptying a considerable amount of unaccounted for cash from her savings account. It was big news for a while. The police believed drugs and drug money were involved."

Roger turned to me. "Sandra Ford, you are under arrest for the murder of Special Agent Robert Wells. Do you have anything to say?"

I turned pleading eyes to Roger. "I didn't kill him."

"Then how do you explain your fingerprints on the murder weapon?" Roger countered, his voice hard.

I'm sure my face lost all its color. I felt like someone had just signed my death warrant. This was news to me. How they could have my fingerprints on a gun I had never even seen was beyond me. I would have liked to know how they managed that one. I guess I shouldn't have been surprised. They seemed to be able to manage just about anything.

They were both looking at me now. I felt like a drowning victim, except there was no water. It was hard to breathe. They had me.

Roger shook his head in disbelief, a hard distant look coming into his eyes.

"Roger, I didn't kill him!" the words came out in a panic. "I never even saw the murder weapon."

"But you admit to being there?"

"Yes...," I sputtered out nervously. "But I didn't kill him!"

Roger leaned across the table, his face inches from me. "Fingerprints don't lie," he told me.

I didn't have a response for that one. I just looked at him, the realization that my one possible ally was gone. We weren't on the same side anymore. I closed my eyes in resignation. Maybe I hadn't felt like I should accept his help, but there had been comfort in knowing he was offering it.

"Take her away," Roger told the officer at the door.

※※※※※※※※※

Clang! The door to the cell slammed shut behind me. I smothered the urge to turn around and pound on the door, demanding that they release me, pleading my innocence.

It wouldn't help. It was a natural urge to do so when one felt trapped and imprisoned. And imprisoned I was. I was still reeling from the sudden turn of events back in the holding room. How did they have my fingerprints on the murder weapon? I never saw the gun—let alone touched it!

What cut deep into my heart was the rejection I saw in Roger's eyes, the fact that he believed the police report. "Fingerprints don't lie," he had told me—and he believed it.

I shook my head. Why shouldn't he believe it? Fingerprints *don't* lie! In his mind I *did* have the murder weapon in my hand and then I used it to kill an FBI agent. But how could he believe I would kill my own flesh and blood? How could he believe that I would kill my precious Henry? I shook my head sadly.

How did they get my fingerprints on the gun? I asked myself. How did they do it? What other evidence would they conjure up? Could they have changed the public records as well, disproving my claim to an inheritance? Probably.

It was my worst nightmare come true.

They were going to get away with it.

They were going to prove in a court of law that I was guilty of murder.

I thought of Roger. I didn't blame him for believing the report. I didn't blame him for believing the fingerprints. But that didn't mean it didn't hurt.

With Roger against me, my outlook looked bleak. I felt like I was in a cave and a boulder had just been rolled in front of the opening, closing off the light, blocking off all air, suffocating me.

A MURDER UNSEEN

Chapter 14

Fingerprints Don't Lie

It was late in the afternoon of the next day when I heard the clanging sound of the door at the end of the hall. Swinging my legs slowly over the edge of the cot, I sat up as I listened to the footsteps walking toward my cell.

"Come on," the officer spoke brusquely. "Someone wants to see you."

He opened the door to the cell, motioning for me to put my hands out in front, palms up. I hated the feeling of the cold metal cuffs against my wrists. I hated the constriction. I hated what it meant. This shouldn't be happening. And yet it was. He took me back to the room where I had been questioned by

Roger.

"Take a seat. Someone will be here shortly," the officer spoke curtly and then went to stand by the door like a sentry on duty.

I sat down, wondering if it was Roger coming. I hoped not. I wasn't ready to see him again.

Hearing the sound of approaching footsteps, I turned toward the door, letting out an involuntary gasp at the sight of Detective Jordan Lewis filling the doorway. He was here!

I swallowed hard as he walked through the doorway. I felt like a caged animal as he looked me over, taking in my face, my hair, my overall appearance. I didn't notice Roger behind him at first. I was too busy watching Detective Lewis and trying to breathe. I felt like something was pressing in on my chest, smothering me. Mortar had just sealed the few cracks where slivers of light seeped into my cave.

"It is definitely her," Detective Lewis said after a minute. "She's cut her hair and dyed it, but it's her."

He turned to the guard. "We won't need you now. My men and I will take it from here."

My men and I will take it from here. It sounded so ominous, so final. It sounded like my death sentence.

My hands began to quiver, my throat constricted with fear, and the blood in my temples pounded. Detective Lewis would not allow me to see

New York again. I was convinced of that. Somewhere along the way, I would have an unfortunate accident. I would be dead before we arrived.

"Detective Phillips, thank you for your part in apprehending Mrs. Ford. I didn't think we were ever going to see justice in this case."

"Just doing my job," Roger replied, avoiding my eyes.

Just doing your job? I turned my head away, shaken by his uncaring attitude. At least yesterday he had been shocked and mad at me. But today...today he just didn't care. Roger didn't care anymore....

I knew it was for the best. I knew it was what I had been wanting—that Roger would be distanced from me. Roger not caring was his best protection. I just wasn't prepared for the sting of rejection.

"Is the paperwork ready?" Detective Lewis asked Roger, breaking eye contact with me.

"The paperwork is processed. You may move the prisoner at any time," Roger replied, his voice strangely void of emotion.

The prisoner. Now I was just another prisoner to Roger—and Detective Lewis was going to move me.

I was determined to not allow Detective Lewis to win. At the same time, there was that overwhelming conviction that sometime today I would die. Even knowing how contradictory those thoughts were, they were equally strong. The thought flashed through my mind that maybe I was on the brink of insanity. I wasn't even making sense anymore.

One thing I determined in that moment: I was going to put up a fight, but not here and not with words. Words weren't going to work. Words couldn't save me. Not this time.

I knew I had to try to escape. The how was the mystery. I would be watching for an opportunity, for any opportunity. I knew I was desperate. I was willing to risk my life to escape, confident as I was that I would lose it if I remained in Detective Lewis's custody.

My hopes were challenged as a guard bent to fasten leg irons on my ankles. I hadn't counted on those. My chances of escape were narrowing by the moment.

Oh God, if You exist, help me, I prayed. It was an honest prayer that came unexpected to even me—but not one I expected to have answered. I had never cared about God up until this point, so even if He really did exist, why should He care about me now? Roger surely didn't—and Roger seemed to have a direct line to God. But, for what it was worth, I prayed. I had reached the bottom.

I walked meekly from the room, watching and waiting.

Pulling away from the police station in an unmarked car, I wondered what Detective Lewis had planned for me. I was so totally at his mercy, but he would have to make it look like an accident. It would have to be something above questioning. If questions were raised, Roger would begin to wonder.

Maybe I was being foolish, but I believed it. If my death looked questionable, I truly believed that Roger would have second thoughts, causing him to latch on to what I had told him, and that he would search for the truth. But by then, it would be too late for me.

As we neared an intersection, a truck veered sharply in front of us from the left-hand lane, forcing our driver to turn down a side alley to miss him.

Cursing, our driver slammed on the brakes just short of ramming into the back end of a white service van that was parked a short ways down the side alley. Throwing the car into reverse, he began to back up. More cursing followed when he looked back to find the truck had effectively blocked him in.

Startled, I watched as three men dressed in black, their faces hidden behind black ski masks, leapt from the back of the white service van. They were armed and their guns were trained on us.

"Get your hand away from that gun!" one man in black barked at Detective Lewis. His gun was aimed at Detective Lewis's head through the window, his trigger finger ready.

I glanced over in time to see Detective Lewis

carefully remove his hand from his jacket, slowly raising them so the man could see them.

A man was opening my door. My seat belt was unsnapped and I found myself being pulled from the car.

Glancing over at Detective Lewis, I didn't know what to make of the expression on his face. He looked genuinely shocked. And yet, I reasoned, this all had to be a facade. These were his men making my escape look real even to the men with him—and then they would kill me.

Still, I couldn't fight them. The handcuffs and leg irons limited my movements. They half dragged me to the waiting van, dumping me unceremoniously onto its floor.

I jerked when I heard a gunshot, thinking it was over, thinking I had been shot—but I hadn't. They had shot out the front tires of the unmarked car. They were making this look real.

One of the men knelt beside me, fumbling with the locks on the handcuffs. The handcuffs dropped from my wrists. I rubbed them tenderly as he reached for the leg irons. His gun was in a shoulder holster, easily within my reach. Glancing at the other two men, I noticed they had holstered their weapons.

The legs irons were coming off. I wondered if it was a set up. It probably was, but the opportunity was too great to pass. As he pulled the leg irons free of my legs, I lunged at him, yanking the gun from the holster, pointing it at him with my finger on the trigger.

He backed up, his hands slightly raised in surrender, and eyed me with a mixture of curiosity and surprise. I would have preferred to have seen fear.

One of the two men with him had his hand on his gun, ready to pull it out of the holster.

"Pull that gun out real slowly with your fingers and slide it over here to me. Don't try anything or I will shoot you," I warned him as I scooted back against the side of the van where I could keep an eye on the driver as well.

Carefully he removed the gun from its holster and slid it across the floor to me.

"Easy now," he told me softly as he sat down against the far side of the van, "We're on the same side."

"What type of fool do you take me for?" I retorted in an effort to mask my fear and confusion. My eyes darted from one man to another. I stood up warily.

"Roger sent us. He's trying to help you," the man continued calmly.

I give the man credit. He stayed calm. The gun was pointed directly at him with my finger on the trigger—and the van wasn't exactly going over smooth roads.

"You'll have to do better than that," I told him, unconvinced.

"Put the sweatshirt on," he instructed me as though I wasn't pointing a loaded and cocked gun at him. A gray sweatshirt lay on the floor near my feet. "In just a few more blocks we'll pull over and you'll get out. There is a gray Fiat waiting to take you to a safe house."

"Forget it. I'll find my own safe house."

"We don't have time for this. They'll be after us any minute," he protested.

"You *are* them! Now take the handcuffs and handcuff your hand to your friend there."

He reached for the handcuffs, but he was mad. He had just snapped them on his wrist when the van pulled to an abrupt stop, causing me to lose my balance. I fell back against the wall of the van.

The man closest to me saw his chance and dove at me, knocking me down. My head connected solidly with the floor of the van. Roughly he squeezed the wrist that still held the gun. Pain shot through my wrist, but I refused to let go.

"Drop the gun," the third man demanded, his gun out and trained on me.

I looked into the end of his gun—and released the grip on mine. My wrist ached. My head pounded. I had lost. I felt sick.

"Look at me," the first man demanded sharply, not releasing his grip on me. "We're on the same side."

I just looked at him in bewilderment. This was where he was supposed to shoot me.

"Did you hear what I just said? We're on the same side," he told me again, more gently this time.

"Roger sent you?" I said slowly. *Could he be telling the truth? If they were Lewis's men, wouldn't they have already killed me?*

"Yes, Roger sent us. We're out of time. Are you going to cooperate or do we need to knock you out and drag you to the car?"

"I'll cooperate," I told him—but I still didn't trust them.

"Good." He loosened his grip on me.

"Here's the sweatshirt," he said as I massaged my tender wrist.

"Sorry about that," he apologized as he yanked off the ski mask and black sweatshirt.

"Let's go," the man by the door called out as he opened the back door of the van. The man nearest me guided me out the door and into the waiting gray Fiat. He climbed in the back seat beside me. The Fiat was moving before the doors were closed.

My mind raced as the Fiat zigzagged through town. Did I dare trust them? Were they on my side? Had Roger really sent them—or were they part of Detective Lewis's elaborate scheme to have me silenced once and for all? I couldn't decide. I didn't know whom to trust.

The light up ahead turned yellow. We would have to stop. Out of the corner of my eye I could see the man beside me was relaxed. His gun was holstered. The driver was intent on the traffic. I made up my mind. Casually I moved my arm, resting it on the armrest, my fingers inches from the door handle. The car slowed to a stop.

"Don't try it," the man beside me spoke conversationally as I reached for the door handle.

I turned to look at him, startled. I hadn't thought he was watching. Obviously he had been.

"Without our help, they'll find you and you'll be dead within a few days."

"Or you are part of Detective Lewis's plan to get rid of me," I countered warily, my hand still touching the door handle.

"You really believe that, don't you?"

I didn't answer immediately. He looked genuine. I shook my head. I was tired and confused.

"I don't know," I told him honestly. "I don't know what to believe anymore."

"Roger believed you," the man told me.

"That's a lie!" I responded bitterly.

"No, it's not."

"If he believed me, why did he turn on me? I thought he was my friend, but he turned on me when supposed evidence came in. 'Fingerprints don't lie.' That's what he told me."

"Believe what you want to believe, but without us you're dead."

I relaxed my grip on the door handle. Maybe they were on my side.

"That's better. You can call me John."

"But that's not your real name, is it?"

"No."

I leaned back against the seat and closed my eyes. The waters were so muddy.

A MURDER UNSEEN

Chapter 15

The Safe House

We pulled into the safe house just after dark. Even so, they pulled directly into the garage, closing the door before letting me get out. Inside the house, I took note that the shades were drawn.

"You are not to be anywhere near the windows when the shades are open," John told me.

I looked at him warily. Was that for my protection or theirs? I took note of the layout of the house. From the garage, we entered a breakfast nook right off the kitchen. The dining room was directly behind the kitchen, separated by a bar counter. Walking further in, I saw the living room off to the right near the front door.

A MURDER UNSEEN

It was a relatively new home and looked more like a bachelor's pad than a real home. The furniture was functional, but old and mismatched—and not in a quaint way. There were no pictures on the walls. There was nothing to make the place look comfortable and lived in. It was, like the furniture, functional.

A man was waiting in the living room.

"So you're Sandra," he said with a welcoming smile. "Welcome to your new home. My name is Larry."

He reached out his hand. I took it, not liking the feel of his handshake, but not knowing why. I couldn't shake the feeling that all was not as it seemed—as much as I wanted to believe it.

"Thank you," I replied, not knowing what else to say. Everything had happened too fast. My mind had not caught up with the fact that I was supposedly safe. *Was I really safe?*

"Would you like to see your room?" John asked.

"Sure," I replied, suddenly tired. It had been a long day. It had been a long week. We walked through the living room and down a short hall.

"The first room on the right is Larry's. The last room is mine," John explained, pointing to the doors. "We'll use the hall bathroom."

He opened the door on the left. "This is your room. There's a bathroom through the door at the far side. You should find everything you need in the bathroom or in the closet over there. If you can't find something you need, just ask."

"Thank you," I told him sincerely. "I think I'll go to bed now. I'm pretty tired."

"I thought you might want to. If you want anything to eat or drink, help yourself to what's in the cupboards and refrigerator."

"Thank you."

"See you in the morning," John told me as he walked out of the room, closing the door behind him.

After a long, hot shower, I changed into the generic gray sweat suit I found in the closet and then laid down on the bed. I pulled the comforter up around my neck and closed my eyes in exhaustion.

※※※※※※※※※※

Crystal! My daughter's face flashed before me, so real, so alive! She was smiling and laughing. She was running toward me....

Suddenly the image changed and she was in her booster seat next to me. Her eyes were round with fear. Her precious little mouth was wide open in a silent scream. She was falling, falling...away from me. Her small hands were outstretched toward me, her eyes begging me to save her—but I couldn't reach her....

The image faded abruptly. It was replaced by the sneering face of the nameless murderer of my family.

He was coming after me now, a gun in his

hand. I tried to run. I stumbled. I was falling and he was nearly upon me....

"No! No! Don't hurt me!" I awoke with a start, awakened by my own screams, my arms flailing at the nameless killer. I jerked to a sitting position, leaning back on my arms. I was shaking and sweating. My breathing was rapid and shallow.

The door burst open and John came in, flicking on the light. His gun was out.

"Are you okay?" he asked as he quickly looked around the room, checking the bathroom and the closet.

"I'm fine," I answered him shakily as I threw my legs over the edge of the bed and sat up. "It was just a dream."

"Some dream," he commented, holstering his gun. John was joined by Larry. I could tell I had gotten them out of bed.

"I'm sorry.... I didn't mean to disturb you," I apologized. I was on the verge of tears.

"Hey, no problem," Larry assured me. "That's why we're here."

I didn't say anything. I knew I wouldn't be able to get back to sleep. The nightmares. They were back. Everything was back—all the terrifying memories, the fears, and uncertainties. I was shaking like a leaf.

"Do you want some coffee?" John asked.

"Sure," I replied, hearing the tremor in my voice.

"Come on then," John said, motioning for me to join him.

In the living room, I sat on the edge of the couch and cradled the coffee mug in my hands. My eyes were vacant, staring unseeing into the distance. I couldn't get my daughter's face out of my mind—nor the face of her killer. He was there with me right then, in my mind, taunting me, assuring me that one day he would get me. I hadn't touched the coffee.

"Do you want to talk about it?"

John's voice startled me. Jumping at the sound of his voice, I spilled coffee on my clothes and the rug. I placed the mug on the table with a clatter and sat staring at it.

I knew I needed sleep. I was exhausted. I also knew sleep would not come. My nerves were taut. My emotions were running rampant. I was past reasoning and I knew that too, in an academic sort of way. I remember wondering how much one could take before their mind snapped. I felt close.

"Are you okay?" John asked, his hand on my shoulder. It was supposed to be reassuring, but it only made my uneasiness multiply two fold.

"I'm just fine," I answered sharply.

He pulled back his hand.

"I'm...sorry," I apologized, dropping my head into my hands. "I'm not usually like this. It's been a long day—a long week—and I haven't been sleeping well at all."

"The nightmare?" John questioned me softly.

I nodded my head, knowing I should be thankful for his concern.

"They aren't going to get you," John told me firmly. "You are safe here."

I just looked at him, unconvinced.

"We won't let them get you," John told me again.

I nodded my head in mute agreement. My mind and heart did not agree.

"Are you sure you don't want to talk about it? It might help," John pressed me.

"Not tonight. Maybe in the morning."

"That's fine. Whenever you're ready.—Do you want more coffee?"

"I think I'll pass. Thanks anyway." I stood to leave. "Good night."

"See you in the morning," John called after me.

Back in the room, I left the bedside lamp on and pulled the covers up around my neck—but my eyes remained wide open. I didn't want to close them. I didn't want the nightmares to return. Eventually exhaustion won and I fell asleep.

The next morning I woke to the smell of coffee. Pushing the comforter off, I headed to the bathroom to freshen up.

Feeling at least presentable, I reached for the doorknob to follow the smell of the coffee—but then

A MURDER UNSEEN

I hesitated. Call it a gut feeling, but something did not seem right. *What was it?*

Straining to hear the murmur of low voices in the room beyond, I realized what was bothering me. When I had initially walked past the door on the way to the bathroom, their voices had been much clearer—but now, it was as if they wanted to be sure they were not heard. They had heard me and knew I was awake!

Putting my ear close to the door, I listened intently. I could just make out what was being said.

"She didn't want to talk last night, though she alluded to the fact that maybe this morning she would be ready to." It was John speaking.

"Make sure she does," a new voice said ominously.

My mouth went dry and cottony. They *were* part of Detective Lewis's plan! They had to be!

"And if she doesn't talk of her own accord?" I heard John ask him.

"Do whatever you have to do. Use whatever force is necessary. We need to know what she knows and who she has told."

I eased back from the door.

"What about Roger? He has to know," I heard John say.

I stopped rigidly where I was, my heart pounding. Fear for Roger's life wrapped a tight swath around my lungs, threatening to suffocate them. I made a conscious effort to keep breathing.

A MURDER UNSEEN

"He will have a convenient accident today," came the response.

No! Not again! I have to warn Roger! I was suddenly resolute, spurned to action.

Tiptoeing to the window, I looked out. The backyard was fenced in, but there was a gate in the fence just several yards from my bedroom window. The problem was that the gate was visible from the dining room window if anyone happened to be looking out.

I looked back at my bedroom door apprehensively. I knew I could get caught, probably *would* get caught, but I had to try. Time was running out. It was already eight. Soon they would be knocking on my door. Quickly, I stuffed some towels under the comforter. It didn't look much like a sleeping body, but at a quick glance, it might buy me a few minutes.

I reached for the latch on the window, quietly unlocking it. The window slid open smoothly and soundlessly. I sighed a breath of relief and climbed out the window. I pressed my body against the wall as I slid the window back down.

Fighting the urge to run, I inched along the back wall of the house toward the gate, careful to make no noise. The hinges were well-oiled and the gate swung open easily.

I entered a back alley. No one was in sight. I stood there, momentarily indecisive, wondering which way to go. Shouts from the house spurred me to action. My heart started pumping frantically. They knew I was gone! They would be here any minute!

My attempt to open the gate across the alley failed. It was locked from the inside. I didn't take the time to try another one, figuring they would all be locked Instead, I ran for the end of the alley and the busy street beyond.

"There she is!" I heard a shout behind me as I reached the street. I didn't look back.

"Sorry. Excuse me! Sorry," I apologized frantically as I ran between people, bumping and pushing, and not concerned by the angry looks on their faces. *They* were not the ones running for their lives!

Half a block down, I jaywalked across the street. A quick glance back told me that they had seen me. They were splitting up and coming after me!

I darted through the revolving door of a mini-mall, racing up the escalator. I hazarded a backward glance. They hadn't entered the mini-mall—at least not yet!

Briskly, I walked toward the other end of the mall, wondering if one of them would be waiting for me there—a worrisome thought for sure. It was then that I saw the walkway over the street to the neighboring building. I nearly smiled, but not quite.

A quick glance back to be sure they didn't see me, and I fell into step directly behind a young mother pushing a stroller while holding her other

A MURDER UNSEEN

child's hand. I hoped they wouldn't notice me. I hoped their eyes would pass me by because they were looking for a solitary woman dashing frantically away from them.

At the other side, I began to breathe normally again. They weren't in pursuit. At least there was no evidence of pursuit. Pausing after I was out of sight of the entrance, I looked around, trying to decide where I should go next. The walkway had emptied into another mini-mall.

A few stores down, I saw a sign for restrooms. If there was any chance of the mall still having a payphone in the mobile phone era in which we now lived, that was where it would be located. I desperately needed a phone. I needed to call Roger.

Despite the intense urge to run, I walked at a relaxed pace so as not to draw attention to myself. Rounding the corner, I could have shouted for joy despite my dire circumstances when I saw a solitary payphone in the hall leading to the restrooms.

I placed a collect call to Roger. I waited impatiently while it rang the third and fourth time.

Come on, Roger! Answer the phone! It's your life on the line!

It rang the fifth time. I wondered how long I had before my captors looked here.

Please, answer the phone! I begged him in my mind while my finger tapped nervously.

I heard the call being answered. I heard Roger accepting the charges. And then he was on the line

A MURDER UNSEEN

with me.

"Detective Phillips," I heard Roger's voice answer briskly.

"They're going to try to kill you today!" I blurted into the phone, my eyes watching the entrance to the restroom area, fearful my pursuers would round the corner at any moment. "They will make it look like an accident. Please, be careful."

"Sandra?" Roger questioned quietly. "Is that you?"

"Yes, Roger, it's me. I know you don't believe me anymore, but please, be careful," I pleaded, the fear evident in my voice.

"Sandra, what do you expect me to believe?"

"I know. Fingerprints don't lie," I answered him bitterly.

"Tell me how your fingerprints got on the gun if you didn't kill him," Roger countered.

I wondered if he was tracing the call—but realized I didn't care. I had to convince him.

"I don't have the slightest idea. They framed me, but I can't prove it.—They put my fingerprints on it afterwards?—I don't know. You tell me. How do you get someone's fingerprints on a gun if they have never touched it?—But that's not why I called. The important thing now is that they are going to try to kill you."

"Sandra, that sounds a bit far out, doesn't it? What you need is to turn yourself in. You are only making it worse for yourself."

A MURDER UNSEEN

"Sure, it sounds far out," I protested sarcastically. "It sounds far out to me that I'm running for my life from people I don't even know. It sounds far out to me that a man tried to kill me. What about him? How do you fit him into the equation?"

"His name is Cameron Holmes and there is a warrant out for his arrest. He has connections to a drug ring," Roger told me flatly.

"And you believe I got in his way?" I asked in disbelief. "You really believe I'm guilty?"

There was a pause now. I almost hung up, but I wanted a response, even though I dreaded it.

"I believe you aren't telling me everything," he answered carefully. "Your fingerprints were on the murder weapon, which you say you never saw. You had a considerable and unexplainable amount of money in your savings account. You tell me what really happened, and I'll see what I can do to help you. But you have to be honest with me first."

"The money was an inheritance from my dad," I told him wearily. "I have been honest with you. I can't do any better than that.—Please, be careful. Believe me now at least. They *will* try to kill you today. I heard them."

"I'll be careful," he responded, definitely not sounding convinced. Then almost as an afterthought he added, "Call me tonight."

"Why? So you can trace my call and bring me in?" I retorted. "I doubt it."

"Please," his voice softened. "Call me tonight.

If I've had a close call today, maybe I'll be ready to listen."

"Or maybe you'll be dead," I added.

"Will you call me?"

"Maybe," I answered indefinitely.

"Just say you will."

"I can't. For all I know, when I hang up this phone I'll go around the corner and be a captive again—or dead."

"But you will try to if you can?"

I leaned my head back against the wall, taking a steadying breath. "I'll try."

"I'll be waiting for your call. Be careful."

A MURDER UNSEEN

Chapter 16

Fear

I spent the day in hiding, looking over my shoulder every few minutes. When I wasn't fearful that Detective Lewis's men would find me, I was fearful that the police would.

Fearful. That one word summed up my day in a nutshell. I also wondered a lot about my sanity that day. I should have been hitchhiking far from there before the police—or Detective Lewis's men, for that matter—could tighten the net, trapping me in, and making escape impossible.

And yet I stayed.

Why? Because I knew that today they would try to kill Roger. If he survived, maybe, just maybe,

A MURDER UNSEEN

he would listen. Maybe he would believe me then. It was a long shot. The more likely outcome for the day would be that Roger would end up in the morgue, and I would be back in Detective Lewis's clutches. There wouldn't be a second chance. Detective Lewis would make sure of that.

And yet I stayed.

It was a slim thread of hope to be grasping for, but I was desperate. I knew I couldn't prove my innocence. I needed help.

My attempt at distancing myself from Roger obviously had not worked. He was already deeply enmeshed in this mess called my life. If distancing wasn't going to help, then I needed his help to clear my name and end the nightmare. I needed access to police files to figure this out, and with Roger on my side that could become a very real possibility. This was my only hope, my only chance.

Sure, I could run again. I could hide again. I could find a new identity, a new job, and a new life—but it wouldn't last. They would find me. Of that I was convinced.

So I spent the day hiding out in a back cubbyhole of the public library, surrounded by imposing shelves of books, and reading microfilms of old newspaper accounts related to the killing that I had supposedly committed. It wasn't reassuring. They had it all wrapped up. I would have believed their story.

My stomach growled, reminding me that I had

not eaten all day. I dared not leave my cubbyhole to venture out where I might be seen.

Looking up at the large white clock on the far wall, I decided it was time to call Roger. I wondered for the thousandth time if he was already dead, the victim of some tragic accident. It was a grim thought, but a very possible one. I wondered what they had planned for him. I stood up and stretched. It was time.

※※※※※※※※※※

Roger answered the phone on the first ring. "I was hoping you would call," he said before I spoke.

"You're alive," I said with relief, realizing that I had been holding my breath.

"Thanks to you," Roger replied gratefully.

"What happened?"

"That doesn't matter right now. Suffice it to say, I had a very close call today, enough to convince me that you were telling me the truth."

"Does that mean you believe me?"

Roger hesitated before answering. "To be honest, I'm not sure what to believe right now, but something's not right.—I *want* to believe you."

"So where does that leave us?" I asked uncertainly.

"Will you meet with me? Can we talk in private?"

"I won't turn myself in," I told him firmly.

"I won't ask you to."

"Won't you be obligated to take me in?"

"Technically, yes."

"And you're willing to go against that?" Roger was the type that went by the book.

"Yes," Roger replied slowly. "Under the present circumstances, I am."

"I'll meet you in an hour at the bus station on James Avenue. Take a seat at the bench by the main entrance and I'll come to you."

"I'll be there and waiting."

I arrived in the vicinity of the bus station a half hour before I was to meet Roger. I spent the time browsing through the stores across the street, an ever watchful eye on the bench where Roger was to wait for me.

I felt uneasy. I wondered if I had done the right thing. I trusted Roger, or at least I told myself I did, but nerves still made my stomach cramp into a hard knot. What if this was a hoax? What if Roger was reeling me in? But he had given his word, and I was determined to trust him until he disproved my trust. I pushed the nagging doubts aside.

Exactly an hour from the time I had called, I saw Roger walk across the platform and take a seat on the bench. I scanned the area before leaving the store and walking over. Everything looked normal, even serene. I felt safe.

He looked up as I stepped up to the platform, his eyes catching mine. They were smiling. I smiled back.

"I wasn't sure if you would come," he said as he stood to greet me. "I'm glad you did."

"So am I. Where to now?" I asked, but the answer was postponed. I heard the report of a gunshot as Roger dove at me, knocking me flat on the ground.

"Get behind that wall!" Roger shouted as he yanked his gun out, spinning in the direction of the gunfire. Another shot rang loud and clear.

I didn't need any encouragement. I was behind the wall in a split second, pressed up against it, my head down low, and my heart racing. Roger was right behind me.

"Keep going! We'll slip out the back. My car is there," he told me as he took a shot around the corner, deterring the gunman. He tossed me the keys. "Get the engine going. I'll cover us."

It sounded like a good plan to me. I grabbed the keys, darting out the back entrance. Roger was not far behind.

We were several blocks away before I noticed the blood on Roger's sleeve.

"You've been shot!" I exclaimed.

"I'll be okay," Roger assured me. "It's just a flesh wound."

"How badly are you bleeding?"

"Not too badly."

I reached for his arm, tenderly touching the area. His shirt was already saturated with bright red blood and it was still flowing.

"Liar," I hissed. "You need to get to a hospital."

"And have them find me there?" Roger replied, his eyebrows lifted.

"They weren't after you. They were after me. You were just in the way," I argued as I started to pull over. "Drop me off here and head for the hospital."

"We're not going to the hospital," Roger said stubbornly. "Don't stop. Keep going. Take the next left."

"Why not?" I demanded, but I kept going.

"I told Detective Graham I was going to meet with you," Roger said slowly.

"You did what?" I asked in disbelief.

"He knew when and where I was going to meet you. No one else knew." Roger's eyes were hard. "We aren't going to the hospital. Anyway, I don't need a doctor," Roger forced a smile. "I have you."

"You need a doctor," I insisted. His coloring was poor.

"You did a pretty good job on yourself," Roger reminded me.

"That was different," I objected.

"No it wasn't. Pamela, this is bigger than I thought. I'm not sure who I can trust. We need to lay low until I can find some answers—and I think you have some of them." He looked at me then, willing me with his eyes to tell him.

"I understand," I replied, shaken, realizing that Roger was more deeply imbedded in my troubles than I had first presumed. It was a relief and a fearful responsibility all at the same time. It might mean his death. On the other hand, together maybe we stood a chance of proving my innocence. It was a far shot, but it sounded good to have someone with me, at least for a while. I looked out the front windshield to escape his eyes.

"Where are we going?" I asked. I wasn't quite ready to talk.

"I have a place we can hide out. A friend's place. He's out of town."

"What about Sarah?" I asked fearfully.

"They left this morning for vacation. A bit early, but safer that way," Roger answered me as he glanced over his shoulder out the back window.

"They left this morning?" I asked quizzically, my eyebrows knit together.

Roger turned to look at me. "I called Ed after you hung up this morning."

"I thought you didn't believe me?"

"I didn't know what to believe, but I couldn't disregard your warning. Whatever else I did or didn't believe, I knew you were convinced I was to be killed today. If I was in danger, I presumed so would my sister and her family."

"I'm glad you called them," I said as I turned left at the next corner.

I couldn't bear the thought of Sally, Ed, and the children being hurt. What was I to do? Would involving Roger in proving my innocence mean dragging Sally and the family into the whole ordeal, putting their lives at risk? Would Detective Lewis take them out, one at a time, until I gave up testifying? A despair came over me. I knew he would stoop that low. He would stop at nothing. And I knew Roger was already involved up to his neck. There had been no choice.

Chapter 17

Unacceptable Risk

We arrived at our safe house, undetected by our enemies. Rummaging through the bathroom cupboards, I found what I needed to clean and bandage Roger's wound. Back in the kitchen, Roger had torn the one sleeve of his shirt off and was holding it up against the wound. The bleeding had slowed, which was encouraging.

"Let me take a look," I told him as I gently pulled the shirt back. The blood was beginning to coagulate. It had been a clean shot. No bones were broken. He would be fine in a few days. After cleaning the wound, I applied salve and wrapped a bandage around his arm.

"We need to talk," Roger said. "I need answers."

"I don't know," I said as I paced the floor. "I shouldn't have involved you in this."

"I'm already involved. We need to talk."

"They tried to kill you today because they thought you *might* know something. Trust me, it's time to play dumb and back out. That's your best chance."

"Did you kill the FBI agent?"

I stopped pacing to look at him. "No, I didn't—but it doesn't really matter. They've already proved that I did."

"Tell me what happened."

"You don't want to know," I protested.

"Yes, I do."

"They'll kill you."

"They've already tried that."

"What about Sally and the kids? Are you willing to risk their lives?"

"That's what this is all about, isn't it?"

I nodded my head, blinking back a tear. "Roger, I've seen what they can do," I reminded him shakily.

"You're talking of your family, aren't you?" he questioned in a husky voice.

"They...they killed them," I answered in barely a whisper.

"I'm sorry," Roger told me quietly. "You told

me not to make promises I can't keep. I promise you, nothing will happen to Sally or the kids."

"That's a big promise to keep," I reminded him. "Maybe an impossible one."

"And I'll keep it.—Now tell me what happened."

I sat down and leaned back in the chair, studying the swirls in the ceiling above me. I guess this was it. I sat up and began my story, working hard to stay detached. It was the only way I would be able to get through it.

"I was walking to my car one night and decided to take a shortcut through a back alley. I know it was a dumb thing to do. It was the dumbest thing I've ever done.

"I was only a few feet down the alley when I heard the sound of someone being hit, followed by a man groaning. Then I heard a man say, 'You didn't think we'd find out, did you?' The injured man said something to the effect that the man wouldn't get away with this, that someday someone would find out.

"I was hidden from view on the other side of the dumpster. I was getting ready to slowly back out of there when I heard the gunshot. The man was using a silencer. I waited until he was gone and then got out of there.

"At the entrance to the alley, I saw a movement out of the corner of my eye. I didn't think. I just reacted from all the pent-up fear inside me, swinging my purse at the movement. I thought I knocked the guy out, but I didn't wait around to see if he stayed down—or to find out who he was.

"I called my husband when I reached the car. He met me at the police station where I told three detectives my story. They didn't believe me. They were condescending, alluding to the fact that I had imagined it all after working such long hours.

"I'll admit I was upset with them. But I was worn out too. We went home. We went to bed. I tried to pretend it was a bad dream." My voice broke.

"You're doing fine," Roger reassured me.

"Henry was so supportive." I turned my gaze back to the swirls in the ceiling as I blinked back the tears. "He got the kids up the next morning and had us going off on our vacation. He wanted to keep my mind off the whole ordeal. I can still see his face when the truck started forcing us to the road's edge. It was my fault."

"Sandra, it wasn't your fault."

"Try telling yourself that when you awake in a sweat from a nightmare of your daughter in the seat beside you, terrified. When you're watching on helplessly—a part of the nightmare—while the car goes over the edge, rolling, rolling and rolling." I was reliving it now. "Then the car hits something and comes to an abrupt stop upside down. My door flies open. My seat belt gives way, and I fall from the car and roll farther down the bank."

I wanted to close my eyes to the horror of

what I was reliving, but I knew from experience that closing my eyes only made it more real. I kept them open, staring past Roger at an indefinite spot on the wall beyond him, lost and painfully alive in the memories.

"Sandra?" Roger called me back gently.

I looked at him as though just remembering he was there with me.

"Sandra, are you okay?"

I continued my story. "I started back up the embankment toward the car. I could see Henry and the kids dangling upside down inside. There was no movement. I didn't know if they were already dead or not. I hope they were, because then the car exploded." I looked back at Roger. His eyes were wet.

"I think that's enough for right now," Roger spoke gently. "We'll contact some people I know in the morning who can help us. We'll find a way to clear you."

Fighting back the tears, I lifted my head. My eyes were moist, but determined. "That won't be necessary. I'm not going to fight. It's not worth it."

"Why? You're innocent! We will prove it."

Shaking my head, I said, "Roger, I've seen too much. I've run too much."

"You're giving up," Roger said tersely. "After all you have been through, you're giving up. You are going to let them win. You are going to let your husband and children's deaths be in vain."

A MURDER UNSEEN

I glared at him then, warning him with my eyes that he was pushing too far—but Roger wasn't finished. He was leaning in toward me.

"And who do you think they will kill next? Someone else will get in their way and they will die. Do you know why? Because you are giving up. Because you don't have the nerve to stick it out and see the real murderers brought to justice!"

"That's not fair, Roger," I protested, angry now. "I'm trying to keep someone else from getting killed."

"You're giving up," Roger said again, his eyes penetrating me.

I stood up angrily. "All right. What if I am giving up? I tried to fight them, but they won. They won and I lost! I can't take it anymore. I'm scared out of my wits. I've been scared ever since that night in the alley. You have no right to sit here and lecture me. You haven't been through what I've been through."

Roger waited for my anger to fade. "Do you really want to let them win?" he asked me quietly.

I sat down again, my shoulders sagging, my head hanging forward, and my eyes closed. When I opened my eyes, I looked over at him.

"No, I don't want them to win. I...I just don't know what to do."

"Let me help you," Roger pleaded.

"I want to say yes...but...."

"Just say it."

"Roger, no! Just knowing me has put you on a hit list. What about Sally? The kids?"

"Nothing will happen to Sally or the kids," Roger tried to assure me.

I looked at him, indecisive. Maybe I was wrong. Maybe I *should* let him help me. What was the right thing to do?

"Sandra, believe me, nothing will happen to them," Roger said again. His words only convinced me that I was right. I couldn't risk it. It was an unacceptable risk.

"No, you telling me that nothing will happen to Sally and the kids won't prevent it from happening."

I stood up and started pacing again. "I'll leave. You can go back and tell them that I nearly turned myself in, but spooked and escaped. You can convince them that I tried to feed you some crazy story."

"They will still try to kill me. They will still believe that I know everything. They know we are close. Sandra, we have to fight this. We have to figure it out. They won't believe I'm not involved," Roger tried to reason with me.

He was right. They wouldn't believe him. I had to convince them otherwise—and only drastic measures would work. I didn't think. I just acted. The gun was on the table within easy reach. I reached for it, cocked it, and shot one round into the fleshy part of Roger's upper leg.

"Now they will," I told him bluntly as Roger let out a cry of pain.

A look of utter disbelief crossed his face as he reached for his leg. I think the same disbelief that I had actually shot him was mirrored in my own eyes. It was time to go.

"They'll believe you now," I said, my lower lip quivering. "I'm sorry," I blurted out before I turned sharply and ran out the back door, out of Roger's life, and on the run again. *Would it ever end?*

Chapter 18

Reasonable Doubt

When I left Roger, I had every intention to give up fighting. I was convinced that I couldn't win—and people would continue to die.

The problem was, the more I thought of what Roger had said, the more his words inspired me. He was right. I had given up. I was letting them win.

Of one thing I was convinced: Turning myself in wasn't how I was going to win. All the evidence was against me and that would be what the jury would see. If I were on the jury, I would have condemned myself. Why shouldn't anyone else?

I determined that the only way out was to be

able to find flaws in the so-called evidence. The jury needed a loophole to let me off. They needed reasonable doubt. With reasonable doubt, I would be willing to face a judge and jury. *But where was I to get such information?* I would have to return to New York and begin to dig. I would have to walk into the lion's den—but not get caught.

That being decided, I blended with the homeless element of the city for several days as I waited for the search to die down. I cringed as I stooped to stealing a clean set of clothes from an unattended dryer in the Laundromat, but reasoned in my mind it was unavoidable. Washing up in a quiet restroom, I changed into my new clothes and headed for the bus station where my emergency funds were stored.

My hands shook as I fumbled with the lock. It wasn't opening. Fear messed with my mind. I glanced up to see if anyone was paying attention to me. No one was. I took a few deep breaths and double-checked the number on the locker. It was the right one. I tried again. This time the door opened.

I reached inside and pulled out hope in the form of a small backpack. Therein lay the funds to run—though this time I was not going to run from a problem, but to a solution. Or so I hoped.

I told myself I was a fool at least a dozen times as I traveled back East, a fool to think I would be able to investigate the murder and prove my innocence, a fool to think they wouldn't catch me. In the end, I agreed. I was a fool. I would probably get caught—but that was a risk I was willing to take.

And so New York it was.

By the time I reached New York City, my emergency funds were getting low. I had spent a good amount on false IDs that should not be able to come back to haunt me. I didn't want a repeat of the Pamela Hunter scenario.

I had enough cash to get an apartment, but I needed a job in order to continue paying rent. Therefore, I needed a job first—before a home. That's what led me to see firsthand how the homeless of New York City lived—and I only semi-lived their lives.

I stashed my money in another bus station locker to keep from being robbed and started looking for a job. Soup kitchens and shelters kept me from eating too far into my savings, though I was getting pretty desperate. Every job offer I found wanted references—which I could not give them.

I finally managed to get a part-time job cleaning house for a couple that ran a retail business downtown. They would let me in before they left for work in the morning, and I would lock up when I left. Those days I would clean the house, bathe, take a good three-hour nap, and still manage to get out of the house long before they were expected home.

A MURDER UNSEEN

That first day it felt so good to bathe, to really wash myself down, and not simply clean up with a wet paper towel in a public restroom when no one was around. I felt human again as I walked out that day, even knowing I was going to pass the night in a secluded corner of the local hospital.

I had become a master at finding quiet public places in which to sleep. With a job now, and managing to wear clean clothes, no one suspected me of being homeless. That was a definite plus in my favor.

The days started getting shorter, the nights longer and colder, and I knew I needed a place to call my own. My break came when the couple I cleaned for gave me a referral to clean house for several older couples in their neighborhood.

I started looking for an apartment as soon as the jobs were mine. The cost of rent was astronomical in the city. My standards lowered each day I went out. I pounded the pavement a lot before I finally found a place that would suffice.

My new apartment wasn't the greatest. In fact, it could rightly be called a dump, but the electricity and water were stable, the door had a good lock on it, and it was what I could afford. I handed over the last of my money for a set of keys to my apartment.

Moving in wasn't difficult considering I had nothing but a small backpack with an extra set of clothes in it to my name. The place came equipped with a stove and refrigerator—but that was it.

A MURDER UNSEEN

It was the easiest move I had ever made. I simply walked through the doorway with my backpack and smiled. I was home. This was my home and I was determined to make the most of it.

※※※※※※※※※※

I can't remember how long I slept on the hard floor, but after a few months of sleeping anywhere I could lay my head, I really didn't care. I could lock the door and sleep soundly without fear of muggers or rapists and that was good enough for me.

In time, I was able to fix the small place up quite nicely. I kept it simple. The bar in the kitchen served as my table. I scoured second hand stores until I found a set of sturdy bar stools. I'm not sure why I bought two. One would have served fine. I was the only one who needed a seat—but I couldn't bear the thought of a solitary stool standing by the bar. It sounded so lonely. I bought two stools and it didn't break me.

My kitchen needs were minimal. I bought a mismatch of pots, pans, and baking dishes at the local thrift store, but chose to be extravagant when it came to my dishes. I wanted a bit of class in my life. I bought four place settings of fine china at a discount store, knowing one set would have sufficed.

A futon went on sale, so I bought it. It was perfect. I would open it up at night and sleep like a baby. It was much better than the floor and tons better than the benches in the hospital chapel.

Beyond that, I bought curtains and a few decorations to make it look homey. I skipped the idea of a TV since that would only call the neighborhood hoodlums to my apartment. I figured if I had nothing of value to be stolen, they would learn that quick enough and leave me alone.

It worked. I had one break-in. After that, they decided I really was poorer than a church mouse, and left my apartment alone. I still had to listen to their catcalls and avoid their unwanted advances, but they pretty much let me be.

❧❧❧❧❧❧❧❧❧❧

As soon as I had the apartment more or less in shape, I began in earnest to try to prove my innocence. I began by pouring over old newspaper articles regarding my case on microfilms at the local library. I even dared to get copies made and began my own personal file at the house. It wasn't anything fancy. I had a simple cardboard banker's box with all the papers filed in it—but that box was a sign of hope. I was determined to find something to exonerate myself.

It didn't take long for me to discover that proving my innocence would involve a deeper investigation. The evidence was overwhelming. My fingerprints were on the gun—despite the fact that I had never touched it. There was no record of my inheritance being passed down to me from my father;

it simply no longer existed in the files. The newspapers said the money was drug money, and I couldn't prove otherwise.

Of course, all this was hearsay from the newspaper reporters. What I needed to know was what was written in black and white on my file at the police station. That would be the hard part.

At first I despaired. They had framed me. How could I dare hope to unravel the mystery behind it?

As the weeks and months passed by, my mind began to turn down another avenue of thought, another avenue of possibilities. What if I could prove Detective Lewis was a bad cop? I decided that was where my hope lay.

I began to make what I hoped were discreet inquiries into the background of Detective Jordan Lewis—always by phone, always from another part of town, and always with some plausible excuse for requesting information.

It was slow going. I knew I could not afford to raise suspicion. I had to be sure no one would learn of my inquiries.

All seemed to be going well. I did find a few discrepancies regarding Detective Lewis. Nothing earth shattering, nothing that would prove him a bad cop, but it was a start. I kept looking.

Life in general was looking up. My reputation as a trustworthy and thorough housecleaner had grown. I had more offers than I had time to clean.

A MURDER UNSEEN

The Hendersons, one of the older couples I cleaned for, offered to rent me the small apartment at the back of their place. Small is how they described it. It was still bigger than the apartment I was renting and with a lot more character.

To say they offered it wasn't the way to put it either. They practically insisted I take it once they found out where I was living. They didn't like the neighborhood where I was lived, and I couldn't blame them. Neither did I.

The rent was cheaper, the place more secure, and the location more central to the various houses I cleaned. It was a no-brainer. I accepted. It was with relief that I no longer had to listen to the catcalls of drunken men when I returned to my apartment each evening.

Of course, having been homeless for a period of time, and then having had to listen to the catcalls of drunken men each evening, this had made me realize how vulnerable I was to assault. Once the money was available, I enrolled in karate classes for the two afternoons a week when I didn't work. The classes were taught by an instructor known as 'sensei' to his students. I was pleasantly surprised that it all came to me quite naturally.

My sensei didn't waste time teaching me unnecessary and fancy moves. He taught me how to defend myself. I wasn't going to win any awards. I wasn't going to take someone down. What he taught me was how to deter a would-be attacker long enough to give me a chance to put some distance between me and the attacker. He taught me how to provide myself the opportunity to escape. More importantly, he gave me back my confidence, something I was sadly lacking.

A MURDER UNSEEN

Chapter 19

Found!

I was late walking home that night, breaking one of my own rules: Be home before dark. I had reasoned earlier in the day that I had made that rule while living in a much worse section of town. Tonight, I had decided to make an exception.

It had been a long day of cleaning. Elderly Mrs. Logan had some extra work that needed doing in preparation for her daughter's visit. I couldn't refuse her. I knew she didn't have the strength to do it herself anymore, but I could have refused her offer to stay for supper. The aroma of homemade stew simmering on the stove had been tantalizing my senses all afternoon. I stayed.

A MURDER UNSEEN

It was a pleasant evening for walking home. The night air was cool, but not cold. Spring was definitely here. I was smiling as I reached the street I lived on. I was nearly home.

He came out of nowhere. I didn't hear anything. I didn't sense anything. There was no warning. One moment I was walking along enjoying the evening air—and the next, a hand was clamped firmly over my mouth and a gun pressed into my ribs.

I didn't struggle. The words of my sensei were predominant in my mind: "Remain calm. Watch and wait for that unexpected moment. Strike hard and then get distance between you and your attacker. You may not get a second chance."

I watched and waited for that right moment, knowing my sensei was right. The element of surprise would only work once. I had to be ready. My life depended on it.

He forced my face to look toward his. In the light from the streetlights I saw his face. It was Cameron Holmes. They had found me again. I'm sure he saw the instant recognition in my eyes.

He smiled wickedly. In that moment I knew he was going to kill me. I also knew I wasn't going to die quietly.

I faked a faint—which wasn't far from how I felt. His hand loosened momentarily on my mouth as my body sagged against him, giving me the edge I had hoped for, the edge I so desperately needed.

Simultaneously, I bit his hand and stomped on the inside of his foot with the heel of my shoe, my elbow knocking his gun hand away from my body.

I swung away, half surprised that I had not been shot already, and that I was still alive. It was then that I heard the gun being cocked. I froze. There was nowhere to go. I turned back around and stood there, my eyes locked on him, willing myself not to show the fear that practically oozed from every pore of my being.

I had felt fear before, but this was strangely different. I had always feared death, mostly because of the pain connected with dying. But this time, Roger's words were coming back at me.

What if Roger was right? What if there was something beyond the grave? What if God really did exist? If He did, I knew I didn't know Him.

Roger had spoken of a personal relationship with a loving God. He had spoken of accepting God's gift of eternal life. I knew I hadn't accepted any such gift. I knew I didn't have a personal relationship with God. I also knew that if all this were true, I would know soon enough, and I wasn't going to be on the right side of the great divide. All these thoughts bombarded me in those few seconds.

I sensed his finger tightening on the trigger. I wasn't watching the gun. I was watching his eyes.

The sound of a gunshot echoed around me. I winced, waiting for the pain that was sure to follow, but nothing came. Instead I watched, confused, as my would-be killer jerked his hand back in shock, the gun clattering on the sidewalk between us. He turned sharply to his right, taking in the figure of a warily approaching man. I saw his eyes swinging back to the gun. I dove for it. Cameron ran.

Lying prone on the ground, propped up on my elbows with the gun held steadily in my two hands, I cocked the gun, lined it up on his fleeing form, and began to tighten my finger on the trigger. My whole body was geared for it. He would never haunt me again.

"He's not worth it," a voice interrupted me, unusually calm under the circumstances. "He's not worth twenty years behind bars."

I slid my finger away from the trigger, realizing what I had almost done. My hands began to tremble. I stared at the gun for a moment before turning my head to look up at the man who had certainly just saved my life. I guessed he was in his mid-thirties, more or less my age. He was of average height, though he looked taller at that moment, towering above my prone position as he was. Or maybe it was his lanky build that made him seem taller. Either way, I felt every bit intimidated looking up at him, realizing what I had nearly done, realizing what he had nearly witnessed.

"I...I thought he was going to kill me," I stammered, trying to steady my hands that were suddenly shaky as the adrenalin wore off. The cool calmness was gone.

"He was going to," the man responded quietly, squatting down beside me. "I wouldn't have held it against you if you had shot him. I saw the whole thing. He *was* going to kill you. He deserved no more than you were ready to give him—but convincing a jury that it was self-defense if you had shot him in the back? Well, that would be a bit difficult. Wouldn't you agree?" He smiled wryly at me, trying to make light of a very serious situation.

"Yes, that would be difficult to explain," I agreed, letting the gun fall limp in my hand. "I guess that means you just saved my life twice. Once from him—and once from myself. Thank you."

"You are most welcome," he replied. "I'm just glad I had my gun on me. … What if you let me take that gun?" he asked, reaching for it.

I pulled my hand back from him, suddenly wary. My eyes showed it.

"I'm a police officer," he said, presuming that would reassure me as he flipped out a badge. It didn't reassure me one iota, but I had the presence of mind to cooperate, handing the pistol over to his care and fixing a relieved expression on my face.

"My name is Jon Cairns," he introduced himself, giving me a hand to my feet.

"Darby Edwards," I gave him my newest identity, one I felt very safe with. I reasoned I should feel safe with it for what it had cost me.

"Pleased to meet you. I wish it had been under better circumstances."

"For me this was the best time to meet you," I told him sincerely. "I'm alive because of you."

"Would you like me to drive you to the police station?" he asked matter-of-factly.

"What...what for?" I stammered without thinking, putting myself in a bad light.

"To report this," he replied, motioning with the gun. "You'll need to turn it in and report on the assault. Maybe you can find his face in the mug shots."

"You're right," I agreed, even though the police station was the last place I wanted to go. "I'll pass on the ride though. I'm sure he's far gone by now. He tried to snatch my purse. I probably should just have let him take it rather than fight him. My mistake."

"And one that almost cost you your life," Jon added.

"Thankfully, you came along. You know, I've had a long day at work. I was just getting home—and now this. I...I need some sleep first. I'll go first thing in the morning." I hoped he bought it.

"Are you sure you'll sleep much after what just happened?" he asked, his eyebrows raised quizzically.

I shook my head. "Maybe not, but I have to try."

"Fair enough. Do you live nearby?"

"Right here," I pointed at the red brick house in front of us. "I was nearly home."

"Oh, so *you're* the new girl on the block," Jon said with a smile. "I wondered when I would meet you. Gary and Connie have spoken a lot about you. All good, I must add."

"You know them well?" I asked, steering the conversation away from me.

"Most of my life. They are friends of my parents," Jon said, walking me to the door. "Are you sure you'll be okay?"

"Yes. Thank you...for everything."

"You're welcome. Lock your door and windows, okay?" he told me as I said goodnight.

"Don't worry. I will," I reassured him, a nervous glance off into the distance. And then he was gone.

I locked the door and windows, then went back and double-checked that the door was securely locked. I leaned back against the door and began to shake uncontrollably. I didn't fight it, but let it take its course. It would pass as it always did.

I'm not sure how long it lasted, but after some time I felt the shock of what had transpired diminishing—and I knew it was time. I took one deep breath—and then another and another until my hands were steady.

Glancing at the clock on the mantel, I figured I had less than an hour before Holmes would be back. It shouldn't take him longer than that to come up with another gun. To presume otherwise could mean my death—and I wasn't ready to die. Less so now that I'd faced death as a real possibility and come away with doubts. What if Roger were right? What if there was more to come after death? If so, I was unprepared and I knew it.

God, if You are there, You will have to find a way to show it to me, I prayed silently. And I meant it.

There was no time to ponder on this new train of thought. I was going to be on the run again and time was of the utmost importance. I was prepared this time. Everything that I needed was in the blue knapsack in the bedroom closet. The knapsack contained a change of clothes, basic toiletries, a driver's license with another new and secure identity, and a thousand dollars in cash that I had saved aside for just such an emergency as this. I was ready this time because my mentality had not been one of *if* I needed to run again, but *when* it would become necessary.

I pushed myself away from the door by a conscious act of the will. I would get ready and I would leave.

Flipping off the porch light, I headed for the bedroom, dressing in record time. Glancing in the mirror as I headed for the closet to retrieve the knapsack, I couldn't help but notice the fine lines around my eyes and the furrows in my forehead. They hadn't been there when I had critically studied myself that morning long ago, the morning after the murder, but a lot of water had passed under the bridge since then, a lot of worries and cares. I let out a sigh of resignation, reached for my knapsack and denim jacket, and walked out the front door.

I stayed close to the side of the house as I headed for the back gate without once looking back. This chapter of my life was now closed. I shut the gate behind me, careful not to let the latch slam shut.

Turning to leave, my heart went cold as a hand grasped my arm firmly. I didn't wait this time. He would be ready. I turned sharply and kneed my attacker in the groin, reducing him to a moaning bent over form. I proceeded to raise my elbows to jab him mercilessly in the back when his voice reached me.

"It's me. Jon," he sputtered between pained breaths.

"Jon?" I stammered dumbly, profoundly embarrassed at this point—and terrified. I'm not sure which emotion was stronger. Why was he here? What did he know or surmise? And what would he think of my leaving? Had I really just assaulted a police officer?

"I'm sorry," I managed to get the words out as he straightened up. In the dim light I could see his face was still contorted in pain. I wasn't sure if I should stay or run. By lack of action, more than a decisive act of my will, I made the decision to stay.

"I thought you were...."

"...the other guy," he finished the sentence.

"What are you doing here?" I asked.

"Your porch light went off. You never turn it

off. I thought you were in trouble.—Now it's my turn to ask: What are you doing here?" His eyes were on my knapsack.

"Out for an evening stroll."

It was obviously not the truth.

"You never planned on going to the station with me, did you?"

"No."

"Why?"

"I don't want to get involved."

"You already are."

"And it doesn't have to go any further than that."

"And the gun?"

"Do whatever you want with it. I'm sure you can handle that."

"You know him, don't you?"

My face flinched ever so slightly, but I knew he noticed. I didn't offer an explanation.

"Who is he? An old boyfriend?"

"It's none of your business," I informed him. Let him believe whatever he wanted. It was better than the truth. "I can take care of myself."

"Like earlier tonight? You would be dead right now if I hadn't happened along."

"But you did happen along—and I thank you for that. He won't get another chance. I know now."

"Don't do this. Let me help you."

"I don't need any more help."

He shook his head, lifting his hands in

surrender. "Okay. It's your life."

"Thank you," I said quietly and then turned to leave.

"You know where I live if you change your mind. The key is under the potted plant on the back stoop."

I stopped, turning to face him.

"I'll remember that, but it won't be necessary. Thank you again. I won't forget that you saved my life."

"Good luck."

I smiled—a smile I trusted looked hopeful—and walked away down the street and out of his sight.

A MURDER UNSEEN

Chapter 20

Shot

"One ticket for Chicago, please," I asked the young man selling tickets at the bus terminal. I really didn't care where I went, but Chicago was the destination of the next bus leaving the terminal, so Chicago it was.

"That will be $118," a bored voice told me.

I doled out the money, received my ticket, and walked over to sit at the bench on the far wall. It was a deliberate choice. A choice made for the view and escape routes. This particular bench was near a side entrance—but with a view of the main entrance as well.

The place was quiet at this time of night, but

A MURDER UNSEEN

that did nothing to settle my nerves. If anything, it made it worse. I felt conspicuous. I would have preferred to have lost myself in a crowd.

Not the type of person to leave anything to chance under normal circumstances, I definitely had not wanted to leave anything to chance under the current ones. I had come to the terminal several months earlier to learn the layout of the terminal and the surrounding neighborhood.

If Cameron Holmes showed up before the bus left, there would be no seconds lost in hesitation. I knew where to run and how many seconds I would need to get there.

Of course, there could always be unforeseen complications, but it was a plan and it gave me some degree of comfort and confidence. Not much, but some.

As it drew nearer to the time of departure, people began to filter into the bus terminal. A young woman in her early twenties came in first, accompanied by a woman whom I presumed must be her mother. The mother settled her in, checking the time of departure several times with the bored man at the counter. She gave numerous instructions for whatever incident might arise during the trip, and then finally, with a nervous glance at her watch, kissed her daughter good-bye and left. The daughter leaned back against the bench, a sigh of relief escaping her mouth. I couldn't help but smile.

A young couple with an infant walked in next.

A MURDER UNSEEN

The wife settled down at the bench closest to the main entrance across the room from me. She cooed to her baby as her husband went to the counter to verify the time of departure.

An older man came in a few minutes later, a small suitcase in one hand, a cane in the other. I felt sorry for him as he shuffled along, alone, to sit at a bench a few feet away. He looked so forlorn. The feeling rubbed off on me.

Two girls in their late teens came in, drawing my mind off myself. Their faces were overly painted, their jewelry in excess, and their clothing skimpy for the late evening chill. Actually, too skimpy for a hot day in August in my estimation, but then modesty had always been important to me, drilled in by what I had at times considered my somewhat old-fashioned father. Now I'm grateful—but not when I was sixteen.

Two young men, in what I guessed were their mid-twenties, came in right after that. They were soon flirting with the girls. It seemed like years since I had flirted, I thought wearily, but my attention was drawn to the entrance again as another man came in.

I stiffened involuntarily as I saw his face. He was looking around the room. Any minute now and his eyes would be on me!

No sudden moves, I told myself. Do not draw attention to yourself!

I pulled my knapsack closer to me, averting my face while I watched his reflection in the window.

His eyes lingered on the girls now, this man that wanted me dead. I wondered if he would shoot me in a public place or wait to do it outside.

Five steps and I could be out the side door and away from here. Timing was crucial. I only wished I knew what that timing was!

The baby in his mother's arms started to fuss, pushing the bottle from his mouth. The mother was lifting him up when the infant did a classic display of projectile vomiting, a good amount landing on Holmes' trousers. Holmes glanced down, annoyed and disgusted, and then turned to glare at the young mother.

That was my chance—and I took it. I was on my feet in an instant. I watched Holmes' every move by the reflection in the window as I headed for the side door.

Reaching the door, I saw him turn toward me, his purpose restored. A gun came smoothly out of his jacket, a fluid extension of himself. I threw myself at the crash bar, throwing myself out and to the right of the door where there were no windows as the bullet whistled through the air toward me.

I thought I had made it, but then felt the sickening thud of the bullet entering my upper left arm, not far off from the last place he had shot me. This was not a grazing wound like the last. My arm felt as though it were on fire, but I knew I would be dead if I didn't move, so I was instantly on my feet.

A MURDER UNSEEN

I could hear the pounding of his footsteps headed in my direction. With my right hand I knocked the garbage can over in front of the door to slow him down, and then raced down the steps to the busy street, cradling my wounded arm against my body.

Needless of the danger of the traffic, I ran out into the street, dodging cars, ignoring the blaring horns, the screeching tires, and the curses calling out to me. Somehow, I reached the far side in one piece.

Thankfully, my pursuer didn't consider risking his life to follow me as part of his job description. My last glance in his direction saw him standing, frustrated, on the far side of the road, waiting for a break in the traffic.

I ran down a side street and out of sight. One block down, I turned left, staggered one more block and turned right again. I stopped just before entering the next street, leaning heavily against the building. My breath was coming in ragged gasps.

I was spent. The pain was intolerable. Any plans for escape were quickly vanishing from my mind. I needed help or I would be dead. It was as simple as that. But where was I to go?

Jon.

His name came unbidden to my mind. I pushed it away. Jon was a policeman. Policeman had a nasty habit of turning criminals in. I was in that notorious class called criminals, whether I was wanted to be or not. He would turn me in. Detective

Lewis Jordan would have me right where he wanted me. And I would still die. End of possibility.

Jon.

His name came back into my mind again as though planted there, refusing to budge. I was getting weaker by the moment. I was losing blood.

Jon.

It didn't make sense, but somehow I knew I was to go to his place.

Throwing my denim jacket over my shoulders to hide the ever-growing circle of blood, I stepped out onto the sidewalk and hailed a taxi.

"Where to, lady?" the balding taxi driver asked.

"Take me to 231 Baker Avenue," I told him, letting my words slur a bit as I settled back against the seat. Better that he think me drunk than injured.

I have no choice. I have got to trust him. I have got to try. I'm too badly injured to run, I reasoned with myself as the driver drove me to Jon's place. Mostly I was concentrating on not passing out.

"Lady, we're there," the taxi driver's voice brought me out of a daze as the taxi pulled to a stop.

"Thank you," I answered, my words slurring naturally now. Handing him a ten, I climbed unsteadily from the taxi.

"Keep the change," I told him as I turned, staggering to Jon's door.

Avoiding the lighted front entrance, I entered through the door to the garage. Hanging heavily on the railing, I climbed the few steps to the side door, knocking feebly on it.

There was no response.

I knocked again, harder this time. A wave of nausea enveloped me. This time I heard movement from inside, and then the door was opening.

"Darcy?" Jon exclaimed.

I felt myself swaying. He reached out to support me.

"I've been shot," I told him weakly as he helped me into the kitchen. It hurt to talk. Everything hurt. The pain was all-consuming. There was only pain and no relief.

He gently eased me to the kitchen floor before removing my jacket. He grimaced as he studied the wound.

"I'm calling the station. This guy is going to pay."

I shook my head, fighting to hide the pain, which was useless. My face was a mask of agony. "Please, no police."

"Darcy, it's my duty to call them. You've been shot. Forget about protecting that old boyfriend of yours." His voice was sharp.

"Please, don't. It will only make things worse."

"Worse than they are already? I should never have let you talk me into not taking you in the first time."

"Please," I pleaded. "Just help me over the hump and I'll be gone. No one will ever know.—And my boyfriend will never find me."

"You want me to fix you up, let you walk out this door, and let that guy finish you off? You really think that's what I should do? Well, I can't do that in good conscience."

"But...in good conscience...you can turn me over...to the police?" I paused to take a breath. The pain was getting worse. Jon was eyeing me, uncertain at what I was getting at, suspicion growing on his face.

"If...you do that...I'll be dead in a day or two," I told him, not wanting to, but knowing if I didn't get his attention I would be just that. Plus, I didn't know that I wouldn't pass out any second now.

"Why?"

"My boyfriend has some powerful connections...even in law enforcement," I lied. It was getting hard to think clearly. I was afraid I would betray myself by saying the wrong thing.

"Having connections may get him off the hook, but it won't get you killed," he responded. "You're a poor liar. I think it's about time you gave me some real answers. He wasn't your boyfriend. Who was he?"

I didn't answer. I didn't know what to say.

"I need some answers. You might pass out, or worse yet, die on me here in my house, which will leave me with a lot of explaining to do. And that guy is still out there waiting for the chance to finish you off. As far as I know, I may be harboring a fugitive from the law."

I winced at his last statement. He noticed and groaned, shaking his head.

"What are you wanted for?" he asked at last, resignation in his voice.

"I shouldn't…have come here. You really don't want…to know," I protested weakly. "Your best bet is to…to take me somewhere far from here, drop me off, and…and forget you ever met me."

"And let you bleed to death." He was a master at sarcasm. He should have been my brother. We could have fought battles with sarcasm. Then his eyes narrowed. "You are going to tell me, or I will call this in."

"It's a long story…."

"Summarize, but start talking."

"They think I killed a man."

"Did you?"

I shook my head, maintaining eye contact. It was imperative that he believe me. "I didn't…kill him."

"How do I know if I can believe you?"

"You don't. And you…you won't once you hear all the evidence they have against me," I responded despondently. I closed my eyes. My head was beginning to feel strange. "I think I'm…I'm going to pass out."

He reached over, checking my pulse. I must have looked so fragile and vulnerable in that moment. I think that's the only thing that made him want to believe me. But would wanting to believe me be enough? I highly doubted it.

"You need medical care—then, we'll talk."

"He'll be…watching the hospitals," I argued, wondering how long it would be before I passed out and Jon would take charge and do whatever he wished. "I'm dead if you…if you take me there."

"You'll probably be dead if I don't."

"Probably," I repeated him. "Nice choice of words. It means I…I stand a chance of surviving. I definitely don't stand a…a chance if you take me to a hospital." I was having a hard time focusing.

"He's only one man."

"But not...the only one." I let out a moan, pausing for the nausea to pass. "Watch your back. He…he saw you. He'll be after you next."

"I'll be careful," Jon promised.

That's the last thing I remember hearing.

Chapter 21

Who Are You?

The first thing I remembered when I came out of my unconscious state was pain, a steady, throbbing, burning pain in my left arm. I let out an involuntary groan. It felt like my arm was on fire and my brain, still foggy, couldn't quite remember why.

I reached for my arm, but a gentle, yet firm hand restrained me. I opened my eyes. Jon was standing above me, a look of concern mixed with apprehension on his face.

"It hurts pretty bad, doesn't it?"

I nodded my head as my brain started filling in the details: being found, attacked but rescued, and then shot at again.

A MURDER UNSEEN

I groaned again, but this time because of the situation I found myself in, not from the pain. I tried to speak, but found my mouth was as dry as a cotton ball. Jon reached for a glass of water with a straw in it.

"Here, sip on this," he encouraged, holding it close to my mouth.

Lifting my head up a bit, I took a sip, filling my mouth with the cool liquid and holding it there for a moment, letting the water soak into my dry mouth before allowing the remainder to slide down my parched throat.

"Thank you," I said, letting my head fall back against the pillow.

I felt as weak as a kitten and that scared me. For the first time in a long time, I really needed someone. I needed Jon. I needed him to help me—but I didn't want his help.

I wanted to run. I wanted to run far, far away and hope they forgot about Jon and let him live. But I couldn't run. I could barely hold my head up.

"Where am I?" I asked, my eyes taking in my surroundings. I was no longer in Jon's kitchen. I was in a bedroom, a bedroom with a woman's touch. Therefore, I reasoned, I was no longer in Jon's house, his being a bachelor.

The morning light was filtering through lace curtains off to my right. An assortment of framed photos were artfully arranged on the oak dresser across the room from me, the pictures obviously chronicling the lifetime of a family. On a matching oak bedside stand to my left, a frilly reading lamp balanced out a family photo in a pewter frame.

"You're at my sister's place," Jon answered me.

"Is that them?" I asked, motioning to a picture on the bedside stand.

"Yes, my sister and her family. She's a doctor," Jon said as if that explained everything. In a way it did, but it complicated matters too.

I shook my head. "You shouldn't have brought me here," I exclaimed as strongly as I could in my weakened condition. There was fear in my eyes, and he saw it. His eyes clouded over.

"Why not?" he asked.

The door opened before I had a chance to respond. A slender lady in her early forties walked in. I knew instantly that it was Jon's sister. I would have known even if he hadn't told me we were at her house, even if I hadn't seen the pictures. She had the same startling blue-gray eyes, the same high cheekbones, and the same full lips.

"So you finally woke up?" she asked, obviously unperturbed by my presence in her house.

"Yes," I replied hesitantly. "I'm sorry about all this."

"Don't be," she protested. "I'm sure you didn't get shot on purpose. Anything for a friend of Jon's. My name is Alice. I'm sure Jon's already told you that I'm his sister."

I smiled weakly. "Still, I'm in your debt."

"No, you're not," she countered with a genuine smile. "Now let me take a look at your arm. How does it feel?"

"Like it's on fire," I told her honestly.

She glanced at her watch. "Yes, it's about time for another pain shot."

※※※※※※※※※

"What did you tell her?" I questioned Jon as soon as the door was closed.

"I told her that someone assaulted you and that you weren't in any condition to be talking to the police right yet."

"You what?" I asked in disbelief. What he was insinuating was quite clear.

"You heard me," he said, coloring slightly. "It did the job. That's all she needed to know. That will keep her happy for a few days at least."

He paused.

"But *I* need to know more."

I averted my gaze, dreading what was about to happen and feeling out of control. I couldn't run now if my life depended on it—and I wasn't sure how little I could get away with telling him.

"Darcy, or should I say, Debra? How many of these do you own?" he asked, handing me two driver's licenses.

That brought my attention back to him with a snap. I should have tossed the one. That would have helped out right now. I had overlooked the obvious, and now I was going to pay for it.

"That's all."

"Which one is the real you?—Or what is your real name?"

My eyes flickered at that. I tried not to react, but I wasn't cut out for this type of thing and the pain wasn't helping.

He shook his head, expelling a deep breath through puffed cheeks. "The plot thickens. Neither are the true you. Let's begin with who they say you killed."

I eyed him nervously. "An FBI agent," I told him and then closed my eyes as his eyebrows shot up and he let out a low whistle.

"Couldn't you have picked someone less high profile?"

"I didn't pick anyone. I didn't kill him!"

"Okay. Okay. That didn't come out right. Let's start over again." He rubbed his temples with his fingers, as though that would help matters. "What's your real name?"

"Sandra Ford."

He didn't recognize the name, I could tell that much.

"Let me hear it. From the beginning."

There was no point arguing. I had no choice and so I began.

"It was June of 2008. I was a happy, contented wife of a wonderful man and mother of two equally wonderful children. I worked late one night at the hospital, leaving after dark. I took a shortcut between two buildings to the parking lot beyond. A bad practice I had. It was a fatal mistake that particular night.

"I heard two men arguing, so stopped, not wanting them to know I was there. Then one guy shot the other. I heard it. I *saw* nothing. They were on the other side of a trash dumpster. I waited until the killer left, hiding in the shadows of the dumpster, hoping against hope he wouldn't come my way. Then I got out of there.

"I ran into someone at the end of the alley. To this day I don't know who it was. A drunk? The killer himself? I don't know. I hit him with my purse, knocking him down. It was probably the gun I always carried in my purse that hit him. And yes, I did have a license to carry a concealed weapon," I added defensively.

"Until this all happened, I was nothing but an upstanding, law-abiding citizen. I had never even got so much as a speeding ticket!

"I called my husband and he met me at the police station. I reported what had happened and was brushed off as a hysterical female that was imagining things. They made a big deal over the fact that I had worked sixteen hours straight before this happened—but that wasn't so unusual. I had done it for years. I did not imagine what went on in that alley. Someone was murdered. Detective Jordan Lewis was one of the police on duty. Darryl Fritz was the other, along with Loren Trent.

"The next morning we had planned on leaving for a vacation. My husband thought it best to continue as planned. He thought that it would be good for us.

"We were in Pennsylvania when it happened. I had fallen asleep. I was in the back-seat behind my husband. Crystal, who was three, was beside me, strapped into her booster chair. Cody, our five-year old, was up in front with his dad. He always loved it when I let him sit there.

"I was awakened with a start when I felt our car slamming up against the railing. We were being shoved up against the railing. I looked up to see a semi tractor-trailer beside up, hemming us against the railing. There was no doubt that it was intentional. My eyes went to the railing. It was about to end.

"I saw Henry's eyes in the rearview mirror. Our little girl screamed then.—We were going over the edge.—The railing had ended." I paused, vividly remembering and reliving that moment, remembering the terror. But no tears came this time. Somewhere along the way I had stopped crying, nearly stopped feeling.

"As we rolled, my seat belt gave way and I was thrown from the car through where my door once was. I rolled downhill, landing under some bushes. Jerking around to look back up at the car, I saw my family dangling upside down in the car. I headed up the bank toward them. The car…it just burst into flames.

"The driver of the semi ran down the bank a short ways, surveyed the wreckage from a distance, then pulled out a cell phone and called Detective Jordan. He told him that the loose end—presumably, me—was tied up.

"I was shell-shocked—so I ran. I withdrew the inheritance money I had in the bank before they realized I hadn't died in the crash. Then I headed south.

"In Florida, I found a woman's wallet in a trash bin at a restroom. I figured I was lucky. It was like getting handed a brand new identity. I wasn't lucky. That was a mistake. I took on her identity, not realizing that she had been murdered—which later came back to haunt me.

"Heading to California, I got a job working as a live-in nanny/housekeeper. I was living a lie, but they didn't know it and accepted me. I was actually beginning to heal. And then they found me.

"A woman had a heart attack in the mall and I responded instinctively. I started CPR, saved her life—and got my photo in the news. I naively thought they would never notice it, but they did. They sent him after me."

"Same guy as last night?" Jon asked.

"Yes, the same guy. He staked out the mall and found me. He shot me, but only grazed me. I was

A MURDER UNSEEN

luckier that time."

"You're still lucky. You're alive."

"Agreed.—I tried to hide the fact, not wanting to get involved with the police, but Sally's brother, Roger, was a police detective and he found out. To make a long story short, I ended up at the police station reporting what had happened. I was back at the house when Roger came to get me. They had discovered I was using false ID and presumed that I had murdered the real Pamela Hunt. I ran again." I caught his uplifted eyebrows.

"Yes, I'm good at that, at running. But Roger found me, took me in, and discovered my real identity. That was even worse.

"Detective Jordan Lewis came personally to bring me back to New York for trial. I didn't believe I would ever make it to New York. And of course, I didn't. He arranged an elaborate escape for me, planning to have me trust his men, tell them what they needed to know, and then they were to kill me—with my death never being traced to him.

"Amazingly, I escaped. This time I ran back here to New York. I realized they were never going to give up until they killed me, so I decided it was time to fight back. I wanted to try and prove my innocence."

"And have you?"

I shook my head. "If I had, I wouldn't be in this fix, would I?—It hasn't been easy. They have the case so wrapped up. They have my fingerprints

A MURDER UNSEEN

on the murder weapon—the murder weapon that I never touched! They have erased all records of the inheritance I received from my father, insinuating that I fled with drug money. That failing, I've been trying to prove that Detective Jordan is a bad cop—without much luck."

"And how do you think they found you this time?"

"I asked too many questions, too fast.—I got impatient.—They tracked me down and almost killed me again. Next time I probably won't be so lucky."

He was leaning back in the chair, regarding me with thoughtful eyes.

"So what are you going to do?" I asked the question that was burning inside me.

"I went by your apartment. You *were* trying to put something together. I found your files. I...believe you."

I relaxed slightly, still on guard.

"But I need your word that you won't bolt."

I didn't answer right away. For all the lies I was living, I really did believe in honesty and in keeping one's word. I wasn't sure if I was ready to give him my word. I wasn't sure if I could keep it.

"I want to check into some things," he continued. "I think I may be able to help you."

"You don't know what you're saying. These men play for keeps."

"My brother-in-law, Ken, is a criminal defense lawyer, and a good one. I want to talk to him. He's gone right now, but will be back tomorrow. But I need your word. You can't run. You wait on us."

"And if you can't help me, I'm dead if I give you my word."

"If you run, you'll be dead. Maybe not today, but one day in the not so distant future they *will* find you and they *will* kill you."

I let out a deep breath.

"Okay. You win. I give you my word."

I handed in my running shoes.

A MURDER UNSEEN

Chapter 22

Jon

The knock on the bedroom door sounded normal enough; the look on Jon's face when he entered was not. His forehead was furrowed, his eyes were hard, his lips pursed together in anger, and his jaw was tight.

"What's wrong?" I asked uneasily, feeling as though a sudden tropical storm with all its fierceness was about to hit me. I wondered if Detective Lewis was waiting piously in the front room, but I had given him my word. I had told him I would not run—and I was bound by it.

"You almost got away with it," Jon's voice was sharp, biting. "Did you really think I wouldn't find out about Roger?"

"What about Roger?" I asked evenly, not

A MURDER UNSEEN

ready to share the depth of my relationship with Roger, not ready to share the depth of knowledge he had of my past, and definitely not ready to endanger his life if somehow Detective Lewis had engineered this. This could be nothing more than a fishing expedition for information.

Jon's look was scornful to say the least.

"Come on, Darcy—I mean Sandra—you killed him!"

I let out a gasp of shock. My face fell. My mouth gaped open. My mind reeled. I had killed him? But how? The wound had been superficial! Maybe it was a trick to make me talk?

"I don't believe you. Roger can't be dead!"

He handed me a newspaper clipping. I read the first paragraph. That was all I needed. All doubts were gone. I had killed him. Who but I had held his gun and shot him? I had killed Roger.

I stood up and walked woodenly to the window. Jon didn't move to stop me. Gazing out with unseeing eyes in the direction of the backyard, my mind tried to make sense of what was happening, at this cruel trick that fate had thrown at me. I had shot Roger to save his life, but instead I had killed him.

I wanted to die myself at that moment. No punishment could have been too great. No punishment would have been sufficiently severe enough to deal with the guilt and remorse.

I turned to face Jon. My face was wet with

tears. "I'm ready to go the station. Turn me in."

It had come to that. It was as simple as that.

He reached for my arm, guiding me to the doorway. I didn't resist. I was numb. I was broken.

His sister! Her husband! Their daughter! Jon, himself! If they are connected to me they are dead! The thoughts came to me from nowhere, the numbness I felt replaced by a new foreboding. A fear grew inside me like a fast-spreading cancer. I stopped abruptly.

"Drop me off in front of the police station and don't tell anyone I stayed here. Don't tell anyone that you ever met me," I warned him.

"Don't try that line on me. Maybe I was a fool once, but not twice," Jon responded harshly.

"You can watch at a distance and make sure I turn myself in," I argued.

"No way," Jon's voice was firm.

"You're a fool if you don't take what I'm saying seriously," I objected. "They play for keeps. They eliminate unnecessary risks—and that's what they'll consider you and your family." My voice was dead serious and something in it reached out to Jon, causing him to stop and reconsider.

"Did you kill him or not?"

"I was trying to save his life." The words came out thick with emotion, my lower lip quivering. "Instead I killed him." I shook my head in disbelief.

"What do you mean you were trying to save his life?"

"Detective Lewis and his henchmen were trying to kill him. He was trying to help me. After they shot him in the arm, I got to thinking that they would kill us both. The only way, I reasoned, that I could save him was to make it look like he definitely was not on my side. So I shot him in the leg—and then left him. It wasn't supposed to kill him! It shouldn't have killed him! The bleeding was controllable," I sputtered. "I shouldn't have left him so soon. I should have waited and made sure he was fine."

"You didn't shot him in the chest?" Jon questioned.

"In the chest?—What are you talking about?"

"The article said he took a shot to the leg, the arm, and a fatal shot to the chest."

"Let me see the article again," I demanded urgently. I had to know! I read the article, the whole article this time, not just the first paragraph.

"I didn't kill him." It was a bittersweet moment. I had not killed him—but he was still dead.

"You didn't shoot him in the chest?"

"No!" I replied firmly. "One shot in the upper leg. That was all."

"The shot to the chest came from the same gun that shot him in the leg," Jon told me.

"I left the gun in his car. What an idiot I was! They found his car and the gun. They found him, murdered him, and nailed his murder on me. My fingerprints would have been all over the weapon. I wanted them to believe I had tried to kill him—but I didn't want him dead! It's hopeless. They can do anything. They are invincible!"

"No, they're not," Jon corrected me. "I believe you. Maybe I'm a fool, but I believe you."

"Thank you," I whispered. It was good to have someone believe me, even if it didn't solve my problems. I was still a threat to Jon and his family.

"What now?" I asked uncertainly.

"We'll talk about it tonight. Right now you need to rest. You're not ready to go anywhere."

I didn't argue.

※※※※※※※※※

By the time Jon came back that night, I had made up my mind. I was going to turn myself in. Not Jon. I was going to do it myself. I was going to distance myself from Jon and then give myself up. It hadn't been an easy decision to come to, but now that my mind was made up, I was determined. I was not going to be persuaded otherwise.

The crux of the matter was the fact that Roger was dead. I hadn't pulled the trigger behind the bullet that actually killed him, but I had killed him nonetheless. I had left him there weaponless and injured to be slaughtered. How many more people would have to die? I was ready to call it quits.

Jon arrived early, arriving before his sister. He walked through the door, a much different look on his face than earlier that afternoon.

I didn't waste any time.

"I'm going to turn myself in. I've kept my word. I didn't run out on you this afternoon, but now you've got to let me go. Drive me to within walking distance of the police station and leave me," I told him firmly, not the slightest hesitation in my voice, my eyes steady but lacking the luster of life.

"You're not making sense. What happened this afternoon?" Jon asked, bewildered.

"I had time to think."

Jon was looking around the room as though someone had been there—or was still there—putting these suicidal ideas in my mind.

"It's the only way to do it," I told him steadily.

"Why?—Because of Roger?"

"Because of Roger," I admitted. "Because of what they did to my family and because of what they are capable of. Because of what they will do to you and your family if they discover you are involved. Who knows? It may already be too late."

"They won't," Jon told me stubbornly.

"Roger said that," I replied, a tremor in my voice. "And look what good it did him! Words are meaningless!—I'm going to do it," I told him, my words almost a whisper now, but nonetheless strong. "I'm going to turn myself in."

I started for the door, but Jon was not to be put off.

"We'll contact the FBI. We'll put you under

their authority—not under the NYPD or Detective Lewis."

"How do we know someone in the FBI hasn't been bought?" I demanded.

"We don't, but we stand a whole lot more of a chance with them than with what you're suggesting."

The *we* was consistent throughout his speech. That had to change. He was not a part of this anymore.

"Negative," I said bluntly. "You still have *we* in your vocabulary. It is I, and I alone, that must do this. That way if it backfires, I'm the only one who goes down."

"So noble," Jon replied, his voice dripping with sarcasm.

"You want to die?" I nearly shouted at him.

"No, but you sure do," he countered.

"I do not," I argued.

"Then let me help you," Jon pleaded.

"I've heard that before. Same dead results," I said cruelly and then walked resolutely out of the bedroom and into the hall.

"You can't," he called after me.

I turned on him like a tigress. "Yes, I can, and I will." I turned abruptly and headed for the front door, my footsteps sure and confident while my insides churned in terror. I knew his hesitancy would not last long. I had to leave right now.

Reaching for the door, it opened of its own accord under my hand. I let go, startled. A man of average height, his look as startled as my own, stepped through the door. It was obviously Jon's brother-in-law. It was enough to break my rhythm. It was enough to give Jon the edge. I had to counteract that—and fast.

"Excuse me," I said politely, a pleasant, winsome smile lighting my face, hoping to leave before his brain took in Jon's agitation.

He nodded his head and moved aside. A confused smile lingered on his face. I almost made it—but Jon was determined.

"Not so quickly," Jon interrupted, grabbing for my nearest arm as I began sliding out the door.

Unfortunately for both of us, my nearest arm was also my injured arm. An audible gasp escaped my lips, my face contorted in pain, and the room started to spin. I was far from healed.

Ken reacted then, instinctively grabbing his brother-in-law and shoving him up against the wall. A framed photo was knocked to the floor in the process. To Ken, I was a lady; Jon was the aggressor. The shock on Jon's face was complete and not lost on Ken.

"Let go!" I heard Jon speaking, an urgency in his voice as he struggled against Ken. Though shorter in stature, Ken was definitely the stockier of the two.

I knew somewhere in the back of my mind, back past the fog of pain, that now was probably my last chance to escape, but my body wouldn't cooperate. I realized through the haze how much pain the medication had been masking. I slid down the wall to the floor. My breath was coming in short, painful gasps. Jon noticed, realized I wasn't going anywhere, and ceased to struggle.

"What's going on, Jon?" Ken asked, his grip loosening, but his eyes looking from Jon to me and back to Jon again. He was trying to make sense of the situation.

"Jon," I spoke out quickly, though weakly. "We've got to leave—*now*!"

"We aren't going anywhere. You're safer here." Jon took advantage of my interruption and started toward me, leaving Ken looking shell shocked behind him.

I stood up with difficulty. Jon was reaching for my good arm to support me. He was there—and then he was fuzzy. The outline of his body began to blur in with the room behind him. Everything became fuzzy. The room began to spin. I was falling—and then there was nothingness. I had passed out.

A MURDER UNSEEN

Chapter 23

Let Us Help

"I think she's coming out of it now," I heard a voice off in the distance somewhere. At least it sounded far off, though something told me it was actually close by, connected to the hand I felt on my forehead.

The feel of the hand was somehow reassuring. I felt myself drifting away again, but then the sensation of pain reached my brain, not allowing me the luxury of drifting.

I opened my eyes. It was Jon's hand on my forehead. His eyes were on me. There was a strange look of pity in them. It didn't make sense. Was there something my brain wasn't remembering?

"You passed out," Jon explained quietly.

I passed out. I remembered now. I wanted to leave, but then I passed out.

"We have to leave," I said weakly, realizing how unreasonable my words sounded. I couldn't even lift up my head.

"You are in no shape to go anywhere." A voice over my shoulder echoed my thoughts exactly.

I turned my eyes towards the voice. It was Ken. "You don't understand," I told him fearfully.

"I *do* understand," he countered. "You are not going anywhere. We are going to help you."

I shook my head. I had to convince him that it was essential that I leave.

"I can help you. I'm a lawyer," Ken told me.

"No, you can't."

"Jon told me your story," Ken said, ignoring my negative responses.

"And therefore, you know the implications of what Jon has been doing by keeping me here. Me. A fugitive from the law. Explain it to Jon. While you're at it, explain to him what the lawless side will do to him if they find out."

"He knows the implications.—So do I."

"Then you know what you'll bring on your family if you get involved. Trust me, I'm not worth it. Take me to some dumpy hotel. Leave me there. Distance yourselves. Then place an anonymous call to the police." I was dead serious.

"And have them kill you?" Ken asked.

"Better a stranger than your own family."

"My conscience won't let me do that."

"Neither will mine," Jon added.

"My conscience won't let you *not* do it!" I spoke out as forcefully as I could in my weakened condition. "I can't live with another death on my hands. Please," I pleaded.

"We have a plan," Jon said simply, as though that was to make all the difference. I had no choice but to listen.

"I have a friend that works in the FBI. We'll get together with him. We'll lay it all on the table. He's a reasonable man." It was Ken talking now.

"Not you. Just me. You *can't* be involved," I insisted. "Let me get my strength back, but not here. Then give me his name and I'll contact him."

"If he received a call from you alone, he would blow the whistle on you before you had time to even open your mouth to speak—and you would be dead." Ken shook his head. "Alone you won't be believed."

"It's a risk I'm willing to take."

"Then you're suicidal," Jon retorted.

"No, I'm not. I'm too scared of death," I responded, thinking of that moment with Holmes, the gun pointed at me, knowing I was going to die, and feeling utterly helpless, hopeless, and unprepared. *Was there life after death? Was there anything after death?* Those were questions I was going to have to find answers to.

"It's already arranged. He's coming tonight," Ken told me.

"I have one condition."

Ken smiled at that. "You think that you're in a position to put conditions on anything?"

I ignored his question. "If he doesn't believe me, you back off, distance yourself, and let justice take its course.—Agreed?"

"I'm not sure if I can. I'm also not sure if you're really lucid at this point. That wouldn't be justice. It would be a crime."

"Maybe not justice for the crime I stand accused of, but there have been four deaths because people knew me. It would be justice for those innocents."

"You can't punish yourself for that. Their deaths weren't your fault."

"You're wrong," I argued, shaking my head. "I may as well have pulled the trigger. I did with Roger. If I hadn't shot him, maybe he could have defended himself. I left him defenseless. You agree with my terms, or I confess when he comes."

"Agreed," Ken responded reluctantly.

"Jon?" I turned to look at him.

"If that's the way it's going to be, okay. I agree with your terms."

"Thank you," I told them. "When is he coming?"

"They," Ken corrected me. "At nine tonight."

A MURDER UNSEEN

They arrived at five of nine. I had already been told their names: Kyle Enters and Jacob Conley. I took a deep breath as they entered the living room. This was it.

"Kyle, I would like you to meet a new friend of mine," Ken said as they walked toward me.

There was a gracefulness to Kyle's step that I hadn't expected in such a wide shouldered, broad-chested man. He would have been the quarterback of the football team. Kyle reached out to shake my hand as Ken introduced us.

"Kyle, this is Sandra Ford.—Sandra, Kyle Enters."

His handshake went from firm to non-existent at the mention of my name. His face changed from smiling pleasantly to a sudden look of shocked recognition at the realization of who I was. He dropped my hand and turned to Ken.

"I thought you told me you had someone who could give me information to solve a murder—not to *meet* a murderer!"

I pulled my hand self-consciously to my lap, grasping both hands together so tightly that my knuckles turned white. My lower lip started to quiver as my eyes were on the pair of men. I felt as though I were watching a drama unfolding before me. This was not going well, not at all. I closed my eyes and wished I were anywhere but there at that moment.

"Ken, I can't negotiate. I don't know what you think I can do. She is wanted for murder."

"For our friendship's sake, at least listen to her side of the story," Ken responded quietly.

"I don't know what she has told you, Ken, but she's a cold-blooded murderer. I'm taking her in now and I'll keep your name out of this—for our friendship's sake."

"Kyle, if you take her in for questioning the world will know and she'll be dead within a few days. When that happens I'll be on your doorstep."

I wanted to dig a big hole and bury myself in it.

"Are you threatening me?" Kyle asked slowly.

"I'm warning you."

"You are that convinced that she will be killed?"

"Yes—or I wouldn't be defending her. All I ask is that you listen to her side of the story. After that, if you can say beyond a shadow of a doubt that she's guilty, she will sign whatever confession you put before her."

"Right," Kyle grunted. "That I would like to see."

"I said I would and I will," I interrupted.

"Why would you say that? To make it look good to Ken? You *know* you are guilty. What's the real game you're playing? You finally can't live with what you have done? Is that it?" He was pushing for a reaction.

"You are right. I can't live with myself. I can't live with the fact that because of me my family and Roger are dead—but I didn't kill them."

"And Special Agent Clay Henson? Let's not forget him," Enters added.

"I didn't kill him," I fought to speak calmly.

"You probably will say you didn't kill Ed and Sally Jones either."

"Ed and Sally?" I repeated him, stunned.

"What? You didn't think we knew?"

I closed my eyes to shut out the swirling of the room, but the spinning continued. I leaned my head back against the chair.

"And the children?" I barely got the words out.

"You know the answer. Why ask?"

They're dead! my mind screamed. *They're dead because of you! You killed them!*

I felt Kyle's eyes on me. I knew what I had to do, but the spinning sensation was back. I needed control, but it wasn't soon in coming. I concentrated on breathing. At least a minute passed. The spinning sensation slowed and the world around me came to a stop. I opened my eyes.

"How did they die?" I asked.

"Oh come on. Give up. Your fingerprints were all over the cutters used to nearly sever through the brake lines of their motor home."

I just looked at him. Roger had been wrong.

They hadn't left in time. Roger hadn't been able to protect them. I closed my eyes.

"Book me," I told Kyle.

"Sandra," Ken's voice was urgent. "Don't do this. Let me handle it."

"I killed them," I said woodenly.

"*You* did not kill them. *They* killed them. Don't confuse the two."

"I may as well have pulled the trigger. They're dead because of me," I told him in a dead whisper, my eyes haunted. "It's got to stop somewhere. It's going to stop here. The killing is going to stop here." I leaned forward to stand, pushing Jon's restraining hand aside.

"Agent Enters, I'm ready to go." I looked over at him, my voice a dead monotone.

Kyle looked at me strangely before sitting down in the chair across from me.

"Maybe I'm a fool, but I see why Ken believed you. I'm listening. Let's talk."

"I don't want to talk anymore. I'll sign a confession. Just write it up. It'll be over. You'll be a hero." There was no fight left in me. They had killed my family. They had killed Roger. They had killed Ed, Sally, Kendra, and the twins. I felt dead.

"Sandra, look at me," Ken demanded gently. "You give up and *they* win!"

"Roger said as much," I replied, a catch in my voice. "Look what it brought him. He's dead. They've already won. It's over. I am not going to be responsible for any more deaths. I tried. I really did. You can't ask more than that of me."

My family! Roger! Ed and Sally! The kids! They're dead! They're dead! You killed them! The thoughts echoed mercilessly through my head.

I shook my head, trying to shake the thoughts, trying to shake the guilt away. It didn't help. I averted my eyes, staring vacantly at the far wall, trying to block out the emotions that threatened to overwhelm me. I tried to stem the flood.

The rush of blood to my head was increasing in strength. My head pounded and ached. I couldn't think clearly. Pressure.... Pain.... Too much loss....

You killed them! All of them! Your family! Roger! Ed and Sally! The children! You are a murderer!

I felt hysteria setting in and there was nothing I could do to stop it. I heard people talking, but found I was incapable of responding.

"Ken, get Alice. Tell her Sandra needs to be sedated," I vaguely heard the words. They sounded so distant. Where had Jon moved to? I thought that his hand on my arm, but if so, why did he sound so far away? What was happening to me?

"Sandra," I heard Alice calling my name. I knew she was there but I couldn't respond. Sally and Ed were dead. Dead.... Dead....

I felt a sharp jab in my arm. I tried to turn to the source of the pain. A needle? My mind whirled. Why a needle? Then there was pain.... Numbness....

A MURDER UNSEEN

And finally nothing but darkness, nothing but oblivion.

Chapter 24

Shock

"She's been through more major shocks in the past few years than a person should be put through in a lifetime."

I was on the verge of consciousness when I heard a voice I didn't recognize obviously talking about me.

"I'm surprised this didn't happen earlier," the voice continued.

I felt distant—not a part of what was going on in the room—but knew this was all very important. What were they talking about? What major shocks? What had happened? I knew I needed answers, but right at that moment I didn't care. I started drifting back into oblivion once again. Oblivion.... Peacefulness....

❦❦❦❦❦❦❦❦❦

The next time I opened my eyes, my first realization was that my mind was clear. The haziness was gone, but what had happened or where I was still remained unclear to me.

Jon. The name popped into my head, followed by memories of being shot. Jon and—what was his name? Oh, Ken—but how did I know him?

I tried to concentrate. I instinctively knew that whatever had happened was important. What was I forgetting?

The FBI! The name came from deep inside me, the name followed by the tragic memory of Ed and Sally's deaths. *They were dead!* The FBI had told me. The shock had been too great, the guilt and remorse too heavy a burden.

"Get Alice. Tell her Sandra needs to be sedated," the words came back to me.

But where was I now? I looked around the room. It didn't have the look or feel of a hospital, though the IV and monitors begged to differ. *Could it be a private health care facility?*

Mulling it over, I reasoned that it had to be some private health care center and not a public hospital for two reasons: first, having worked in public health facilities, I could vouch that this was not one; and second, if I were in a public facility my capture would be public knowledge and I would be dead. The fact that I was still alive was all the proof I really needed.

I tried to sort out fact and fiction. I seemed to remember that Agent Enters was ready to listen in the end. Or did I really remember that? It was all a bit of a foggy memory—like a dream—or a nightmare.

"You're awake," a cultured voice startled me out of my private thoughts. I had not noticed him enter. My eyes took in the stethoscope hanging loosely around his neck, the name tag that read Dr. Harlow, and then my eyes met his. They were gray and friendly.

"How do you feel?"

"Fine…I think."

"Do you remember how you got here?"

"No, I don't. I vaguely remember being sedated, but after that, nothing."

"Rest assured that you are in fine hands now. You are safe here."

That caught my attention. What did he mean to imply by my being safe here? What and how much did he know regarding me?

"And what am I safe from?" I was testing the waters, my eyes intent on his.

He smiled then, a broad smile that reached his eyes. "You are quite lucid now, aren't you?"

"Yes, and you are avoiding my question." I smiled back at him.

"You are in a private room in a private health center where no one would think to look for you—and where no one can enter without signing in."

I looked at him oddly now, a dawning of understanding coming to me.

"And no one can leave either?"

He smiled again. It was probably the closest to an acknowledgment that I was going to get.

"They locked me up in a loony bin?" I asked incredulously. "I might have spaced out, but I didn't go over the edge," I assured him, keeping the anxiety I felt out of my voice.

"I can see that now," he admitted.

"But you weren't so sure before?"

"You were sedated when they brought you in. I handle cases for the FBI. Sensitive cases. They cleared me to see your records."

My eyes clouded with shame and remorse. He noticed.

"They told me your version as well. I wondered if, under the circumstances, maybe you had gone 'over the edge' as you put it. The brain is a very delicate piece of machinery. It can be overloaded. It can short out."

"Mine didn't," I assured him.

"I would tend to agree with you."

"Thank you."

"The question now is whether you are up to talking with Agent Enters—or do I hold him off for another day or so?"

I didn't answer too quickly, nor too slowly. I wanted him to recognize that I had thought about it, but had no need to labor over it. I wanted him to view me as a rational human being.

"I would feel better if I could have a shower, a fresh set of clothes, and a cup of coffee first."

"Of course," he replied. "That will be arranged."

※※※※※※※※※

Two hours later I was sitting in a private office. Agent Enters and Agent Conley sat across from me. Ken sat beside me. *My lawyer.* That is what he called himself. I told him I had nothing to pay him with. He said money didn't matter.

"Dr. Harlow said you remember being sedated," Agent Enters said.

"Yes, I do. And I remember why I temporarily spaced out. I remember about Ed and Sally, though I still can't comprehend it. I feel like I'm dying inside—but I am mentally sound," I answered the unspoken question.

"Are you ready to answer some questions?"

"Yes."

"May I record this?" Enters asked, a question that had only one answer. I gave it to him.

"Could you please state your name." The digital recorder was running.

"Sandra Ford," I spoke into the microphone.

"Your date of birth," he prompted.

A MURDER UNSEEN

"April 9th, 1979."

"Please start at the beginning and tell me everything that happened," Enters instructed me.

I looked over at Ken. He nodded his encouragement. I turned toward the microphone. It was waiting. They all were.

"In June of 2008, I finished work at 11:00 p.m. I started to walk into a dark alley between two buildings to reach the parking lot behind. It was a shortcut and one I had taken a dozen times. Still, it was a dumb move. Everyone thinks they are invincible—until something happens.

"I was a short way down the alley when I heard two men arguing. I heard one of the men say, 'You won't get away with this. Someone will find out, someday.' The other man responded by saying, 'Maybe, but not today.'

"I had stopped, unsure of what I should do. The sound of a bullet thudding into flesh made up my mind for me. I eased back against the wall behind one of those big trash disposal containers. I could hear the body sliding to the ground on the other side. I didn't dare breathe or move.

"I waited for him to leave. He did—and thankfully not in my direction. I thought I was fortunate, but that was only the beginning...."

I went on, explaining how I knocked someone out at the end of the alley, how my husband met me at the police station, and how Detective Jordan Lewis brushed me off as an irrational, overworked female and sent me home.

I relived the horrors of the day that followed as I told them of our car being forced off the road, the fear in my daughter's eyes, how I alone was thrown from the car—and how I watched as my family perished in the flames.

They waited patiently as I dried my eyes, composing myself, and continued.

I told them of my escape, how I found my new identity from a bottle of dye and a discarded wallet. I told them how I moved to California where I later began working for Ed and Sally Jones.

By the time I had told them everything I could think to tell them, I felt spent. It had been emotionally draining. I felt as though I were reliving the memories in the telling of them. The recording was still running.

"You are a lot more confident this time. A lot calmer," Kyle stated the fact, though you could hear the question in his voice.

I shook my head in disbelief. "You would have been more favorably impressed—convinced, maybe I should say—if I had lost it again? Or maybe you think yesterday was an act to convince you of my innocence?" I raised my hands in surrender. "I can't win."

Kyle's eyebrows raised. I knew I had hit the nail on the head.

"I wasn't quite myself the other day. Besides having been shot, I was still weak and on Valium. I was not emotionally, psychologically, or physically strong enough to handle the emotional trauma of learning of the Joneses' deaths." I swallowed hard. "I had only learned of Roger's death the day before. It wasn't an act. My body simply shut down, unable to deal with it all at that moment."

"But now you can?"

"On the surface? Yes, I can. But deep down inside? I don't know if those scars will ever heal. Even if you clear my name, I'll still have to live with the guilt. Eight people are dead. Dead only because they knew me. Despite the fact that I know in my head that I am innocent, my heart tells me that I'm guilty. I am the reason for their needless deaths."

His eyes were sympathetic, but I didn't know what to really expect from him. He had switched from condemning judge, to a listening ear, to interrogator, and back to sympathetic again. Was it all an act? What *was* he thinking? There had been no encouraging words of confirmation—but there had been no words of condemnation either. *Where did I stand?* I did not know.

The digital recorder was turned off. Agent Enters leaned back in his chair, studying me. I wondered if he knew what I was thinking. I surely wished I knew what *he* was thinking.

"My gut instinct tells me that you are innocent," he said after a long while. There was no promise here. It was just his gut instinct.

"But there is the evidence to consider," I

spoke my thoughts aloud, wearily.

"I couldn't have put it better myself," Kyle responded.

"From a quick investigation, you had a spotless record before all this. Yes, you ran. You did take money that, though there's no evidence it was an inheritance, there's no real evidence that it was drug money either. That part was speculation only.

"Everything you have told us falls in place with what we already know, but the case against you is strong; the evidence irrefutable."

"But it's all a lie!"

"But how do you convince a jury?"

"Like you were convinced?"

"If you tell your story, you'll get sympathy, but the prosecutor will be out to make you look bad—and he has a lot to work with.

"If you start calling Detective Lewis a collaborator with the murderer of your family, you will be opening a can of worms that you can't prove. It will be called inadmissible. It would be your word against his and you won't win."

"So we gather proof," I countered.

"Easier said than done," Enters responded.

"We set a trap for him."

"How?"

"Can you access his files, bank accounts, and telephone records—without his knowledge?" Those were all the things I had wanted access to, but couldn't.

"Why?"

"There has got to be something there. There has got to be some connection that's dubious, some unexplainable sums of money...something."

"Dubious won't stand up in court."

"But Detective Lewis caught in the act of trying to keep me quiet would dispel doubts. We glean enough dubious connections or transactions, then I call Detective Lewis and convince him that I have enough evidence to open an investigation. I'll convince him that I will expose him unless he pays me."

"He won't fall for it."

"He will. He'll jump at the chance to meet me in person for the exchange."

"Right. So he can kill you."

"That's a given—that he'll try. I figured it would be your job to make sure he didn't succeed."

"Bad idea. Scrap it," Ken said.

"Risky, but not bad," I countered, a smile on my face. It was a strange smile of hope.

"You are crazy," Enters said, looking at the smile on my face, a frown on his.

"Don't say that when the dear doctor returns. I don't want to make my stay here permanent," I answered, still smiling. "I am not crazy. I'm hopeful. Come on. This is my chance! I can prove he's guilty if he falls for it."

"More likely he'll kill you, saying he caught you and you pulled a gun on him."

"But *you* know!" I protested.

"Not good enough."

"Okay," I said, my brain racing for the right answers. I knew they were there. "My phone call can be recorded. A wire on me when I go in. You'll have a recording of all that is said."

"And he could still kill you," Kyle's broken record continued.

"I'll cover myself. I'll tell him once I meet him that if anything happens to me, that if I don't show up at a specific place by a specific time, that three sealed packages will automatically be mailed: one to the NYPD, one to the FBI, and one to the New York Times."

"You have thought this through and you are determined to do it, aren't you?" Agent Enters said.

"Actually, I've been making it up as I've gone along," I admitted. "But I *am* determined."

Enters chuckled at that. "We'll think about it. I'm not sure if I can get the approval to go ahead."

"Why not?" I asked. My face sagged, the reason becoming clear to me. *Why should they trust me out of their sight?* "I won't run," I told him, my eyes steady.

He didn't say anything. He just looked at me.

"Why would I run when I finally get a chance to prove I am innocent? That doesn't make sense. I'm *sick* of running."

"My boss won't believe you." He paused.

From the look on his face I knew more bad

news was coming.

"It was his partner you supposedly murdered."

I groaned. "Then why did you even bother to listen to me?"

"Your boss doesn't know yet," Ken spoke up, his meaning obvious.

Kyle nodded his head, chewing thoughtfully on the end of his pen. "True," was all he said.

After a few moments of deliberation, Kyle looked over at his silent partner. At least that is what I had labeled his partner in my mind. Silent partner nodded his head slightly.

"Tonight then," Kyle said, a look of determination in his eyes.

I looked from man to man, a confused look on my face. I hadn't understood the silent exchange.

"What about tonight?" I asked uncertainly.

"You are going to break out of here."

"And how am I to break out? And where to?"

"After supper tonight, when the next shift of nurses come on duty, the fire alarm will go off. During the confusion of the change in shifts, compounded by the fire alarm, you will rush out of your room. A male nurse will be waiting by your door. His name tag will read Dale Jones. He will get you out and take you to a waiting car."

"When did you think this one up?" I asked.

"Actually, I've been making it up as I've gone along," he mimicked me.

I chuckled.

"I guess I'm off on an adventure tonight."
"Have some faith. We'll take care of you."

A MURDER UNSEEN

Chapter 25

Escape

Alone in my room, I had time to think. Though my mind accepted the fact of the Jones and Roger's deaths, my heart didn't want to believe it. How could my worst nightmare have come true?

The strange realization came that, though I grieved for them, I had no doubts of where they were. They were in heaven. There was also the realization that I knew, that if Holmes had succeeded in killing me on any of his numerous attempts, that I would not have joined them.

When Roger shared the salvation message with me, he had explained how God's gift of eternal life was based on the redemptive act of His Son,

A MURDER UNSEEN

Jesus, who came to earth in the form of a mere man and lived a sinless life.

Roger had explained how Jesus died as the perfect, sinless sacrifice. He had made it clear. God had done it all. There was no "doing" necessary on my part. I had only to believe and accept God's gift of grace.

Yet, despite the fact that Roger had explained it clearly, I had not been ready. I couldn't see accepting God's gift of grace and then keeping on living a lie—and I didn't see a way out of my circumstances.

Then I had faced certain death. I had looked death in the eye when Holmes had his gun aimed for my chest, his finger pulling on the trigger. I heard the shot. I thought that was the end, and in that moment Roger's words came back to me: "Don't wait too long."

In that split second I knew I had to do something about what Roger had shared with me, but then Jon was there and everything happened so fast. There had been no time to think, but in that brief moment of insight, I had asked God to show me He was real. I was open then. Now I was convinced.

Only a miracle could have resulted in my being rescued by Jon, and subsequently, being put in contact with Special Agent Kyle Enters. Only a miracle could have made it possible that Agent Enters would listen to a fugitive's story.

God had worked out a way for me to quit

living a lie. The final outcome still stood on shaky ground, but I was going to take advantage of the situation God had placed me in. Somehow, I could not shake the belief that it was all going to work out. It was a crazy thought under the circumstances, but four times now I should have died at the hands of my enemies, and four times my life had been spared.

Coincidence?—Hardly. No one was that lucky. It had to be God—and He had to have a reason behind it. I closed my eyes, saying the first real prayer of my life.

"God, You are real. Of that I am convinced. I believe that now. I know I'm a sinner, undeserving of your love and grace. Yet, You sent Your Son, Jesus, to pay the price for me, to die in my place. Thank you."

Nothing changed—and yet everything changed in that moment. I was still Sandra Ford, wanted for murder. I was still facing life imprisonment at best, death at worst if my situation were not resolved, but suddenly there was no more fear. Fear had been pushed aside by a strangely out-of-place feeling of peace.

"Thank you, Father," I mouthed the words as a tear escaped from the corner of my eye, landing on my cheek. Someone cared for me. I was no longer alone.

A MURDER UNSEEN

Supper was excellent—I think. It looked good anyway: slices of roast beef, mashed potatoes with gravy, cream-style corn, and a dinner roll.

I ate, though hardly tasting it. My mind was miles away. My mind was consumed by two very different things, yet both being monumental in my life at that moment. My mind was consumed by the upcoming escape—and the awe of my salvation.

The nurse's aid came in and removed the dinner tray. My anticipation grew. Any time now and the nurses' shift would change. Any time now and the fire alarm would be sounded. Any time now and I would escape this place!

My street clothes felt bulky under my hospital issue pajamas. Once we were out of sight of the hospital staff, I was to get rid of the pajamas in order to escape.

I felt like a child again, ready to sneak out of the cabin after lights out. How many years ago had that been? In some ways, it seemed like yesterday.

It had been the summer my father was stationed in San Diego, California. He had sent me to summer camp after I had *begged* him to send me. I had made a friend during that school year, my first really close childhood friend. I was 10 and Mandy Koenig was 12. She was two years my senior and in my estimation, oh, so cool. When she got new Levis, I wanted them. But it went two ways. When I got new Reeboks, she had to have them also. She was going to this summer camp way up in Montana, a camp in the mountains. I *had* to go! And my father sent me.

We sneaked out of the cabin after lights out, not to commit some heinous crime, but to TP the boys' cabin while they were on an overnight camping trip. We didn't get caught.

God, let that be true of tonight. Don't let me get caught. I smiled. I could pray now. I had someone on my side. I could talk to God.

❦❦❦❦❦❦❦❦

Even knowing the alarm would ring, I was not prepared for the shrill sound. My heart started to race when I heard it. I stood up quickly and hurried for the door.

Plastering the appropriate mask of fear on my face, I became just one more confused, scared patient filling the hall that had been vacant but a moment earlier.

I glanced around for Dale Jones, the male nurse who was to guide me to the waiting car, but he wasn't there. The scared and confused look on my face became real. *What had gone wrong?*

My heart pounded with desperation as I milled toward the double doors at the end of the hall that I had been told were always locked. Now they unlocked and the fearful crowd was pushing through the open doors into the hallway beyond that would eventually empty into the lobby—and freedom.

Nurses were trying to stay calm as they urged

those of us who could manage alone to head for the main entrance. Behind the forced calmness, I could feel their fear. Fire was foremost in their minds. They wondered where the fire had started, where it was now, and how much time they had to get the residents clear of the building.

I had more immediate concerns. Dale Jones was nowhere in sight. There were no male nurses on the floor. Should I still try to escape? If so, where to?

Father, help me! What do I do? I cried out to the Lord as I faced the first trial of my newfound faith.

After passing through the first set of double doors, another set loomed ahead, the ones that would empty into the main lobby.

Call it instinct. Call it a whim. I called it God. As I passed a set of double doors off to the side, I slipped through them, unnoticed in the confusion. I just *knew* I was supposed to.

I found myself in a corridor lined with doctors' offices. Being past hours, the corridor was empty of life and the main lights off. The hall was eerily lit by the red EXIT light at the far end of the hall.

I quickly shed the hospital pajamas, stuffing them in the maintenance closet halfway down the hall. I wanted to run for it, but knew I needed to conserve my strength. I wasn't sure what lay beyond. I was to find out shortly.

I pushed on the crash bar slowly, easing the

door open a crack at first, taking a peek outside. The flashing lights and noisy sirens of fire trucks met my eyes, but no one was looking in my direction. All eyes were on the front of the building, watching the scared patients being ushered out the front door where they were kept together by paramedics. That was to my right.

I slid out the door, and staying close to the wall, turned left, walking toward the back of the building. People were hurriedly moving cars, their attention on their own fears and concerns and not on me.

It was then I noticed the flames. I stopped, stunned. They really had started a fire! An outbuilding, but dangerously close to the main facility, burned brightly. Fire fighters were hard at work. But there was no Dale Jones.

What do I do now? I prayed.

I looked around. No one was taking any notice of me. I headed for a car at the far end of the parking lot, near a hedge. Passing the car, I quickly pushed my way between a break in the hedge and into the quiet residential area beyond.

I stood there, hesitation in my stance. What was I to do? Should I hightail it out of there, forget Jon, forget Ken, forget the FBI—or finish what had been started?

I started to walk down the sidewalk, away from the fire and confusion. I realized that there really was no decision to make. There really was no

A MURDER UNSEEN

choice. The decision had been made back when I told my side of the story to Enters. The decision had been made when the plan was formulated on the fly in my mind. I was going to carry through with it. The decision was irreversible. I had told Agent Enters that if they let me go to trap Detective Lewis, that I would not run. I had meant it. Inadvertently they had let me go. Why? What had happened? I wasn't sure.

Of one thing I was certain. Now that I was right with God, I wanted to do what was right by Him. This time, to run would not be right. Keeping my word was.

However, knowing I needed to contact Enters did not solve my immediate problem. It was dusk, and I was alone in a residential area of town with no money, no ID, no phone in sight, and no place to go. There may have been a gas station or convenience store on the other side of the hospital, but I couldn't risk going near there.

I headed deeper into the residential area, passing an elderly couple out for an evening stroll, and then a few joggers. The evening chill was setting in, and I was ill prepared for it.

Wrapping my arms tighter around me as I stood on the curb at a corner, I wished they had left me a jacket as well as street clothes—but that would have been difficult to hide. I tried to think. I had only been walking for about 15 minutes, but already I felt spent. I wasn't up to this and I knew it. I needed to rest.

A MURDER UNSEEN

It was then that my eyes fell on the house at the corner diagonally from where I stood. Not so much on the house, as on the large maple tree in the backyard, and the tree fort I could see resting in its large limbs.

I smiled. It would be chilly, but it would be a place I could lay down and rest. I needed that more badly than I was ready to admit.

I crossed the street, looking both ways to make sure no one was observing me. At the corner lot I started to pass the house, then slipped off the sidewalk and walked up behind the tree. Thankfully, the ladder was on the far side, out of sight from the street.

I leaned against the tree, my eyes watching the house for signs of life, my ears straining to listen. The lights were on, but I could see no one.

I heard the voices first, the distant sounds of a man laughing and kids squealing with delight. Then I saw them through the large picture window as they came into view. A husky man with curly blond hair was crawling on his knees. Two young children were squealing on his back.

I caught my breath as I was transported back in time to Henry doing just that with our young children. I could visualize it now: Cody and Crystal clinging to their father's back as he raced on hands and knees around the living room. Our living room. Our house. Our life. Destroyed—and what for? I wish I really knew.

A MURDER UNSEEN

In a melancholy state, I began my ascent to the tree house. The children were in their pajamas. They would not be coming back out tonight.

It was only four steps up, but by the time I reached the fort I was breathing heavily. My arm protested from its overuse—and I had no medication to ease the pain.

I lay on the wooden floor, holding my throbbing arm. The half walls blocked more of the night air than I initially thought they would. For that I was thankful. I closed my eyes and waited for the pain to subside. After a while it did, and I succumbed to sleep.

Chapter 26

Loyalty

The golden rays of the morning sun shining in on my face woke me the next morning. It had been a long night. I had slept off and on, but not enough, not as much as I needed. But this was not the morning to sleep in. Who knew when the children might decide to come out and play. To be discovered could be fatal.

The sound of car starting made me peek through the cracks in the wall boards. A car was pulling out of the garage. I watched in relief as it rolled past me, the mother at the wheel and both children strapped in the backseat. One less worry for the day.

A MURDER UNSEEN

I rolled over onto my back and let out a sigh of relief. I wondered what had gone wrong the night before. Were they looking for me? How could I best contact them?

God, I'm scared, I admitted, *I'm not sure if they are for me or against me. I'm just not sure. But I can't deny that somehow I know or believe that You are in all this, bringing my life into contact with these very people. That's all I have to go on. Help me now to carry through despite my misgivings, despite my fears.*

I sat up, suddenly feeling the urgent need to get moving. What if they took my disappearance as an admission of my guilt? I needed to make a phone call as soon as possible.

Despite the urgency I felt, I eased out of the tree slowly, not wanting to risk getting my arm throbbing again. Then I began to walk.

❦❦❦❦❦❦❦❦❦

Thirty minutes later I entered a convenience store.

"Do you have a phone?" I asked politely.

"Pay phones are out back by the restrooms," the woman behind the counter informed me.

I went out back and placed a collect call to Special Agent Kyle Enters at the FBI. The phone rang several times before anyone picked it up.

"Collect call for Special Agent Kyle Enters from Debra Wental," the operator said.

I had given the name on my newest ID, hoping Jon had shown it to Kyle.

"From whom?" I heard Kyle ask.

"Debra Wental," the operator repeated slower this time with exaggerated pronunciation. "Do you accept or not?"

Kyle hesitated before accepting. He obviously didn't recognize the name.

"Thank you for accepting the call," I spoke without giving him a chance to speak. My sweatshirt was held over the mouthpiece, effectively muffling my voice. I didn't want to answer any questions. I knew what I wanted to say and then I would hang up. I didn't know who else might be listening.

"I would like to meet you. I have some information that I believe you would be interested in that I can't reveal over the phone. Meet me at the Harvey's on 12th Avenue. Be there by nine. Sit in the booth away from the front window. Come alone. I'll come to you. If you don't show, I'll presume you are not interested."

I hung up quickly. It was eight now. I had an hour and a half to waste. The Harvey's was just across the street from me. So was a Wal-Mart. It was as good a place as any to pass the time.

By nine o'clock, I was watching from the front of the Wal-Mart to see who would arrive at Harvey's. Several older couples pulled in. A young mother walked up with a baby stroller.

At nine fifteen, a blue Toyota Camry pulled in

next to the elderly couple's Cadillac. A man of medium build and height climbed out. It wasn't Enters.

Exactly at nine twenty-five, a gray Fiat pulled in. The man that stood up beside it, his eyes scanning the inside of the Harvey's, was definitely Enters. I waited for him to walk in before heading across the parking lot, angling toward the back of the Harvey's, out of Agent Enters' line of vision.

Walking down the far side, I entered on what I hoped was his blind side. It was. I was standing beside him before he saw me.

"What happened?" I didn't waste time or words.

"Debra?" Enters said amicably. "Nice name."

"You wanted me to advertise my name? I didn't know who might be listening."

"No, you did the right thing," he spoke quietly. "Sit down. I'm sure you're hungry." He motioned to the food across from him. He had ordered for two. I was hungry, but I wasn't ready to sit down yet.

"Where was Dale Jones? What happened?"

"Relax," Kyle said in a low voice, but it was a command.

"Relax? That would be easier to do if I had some answers. Where was Dale Jones? What happened?" I demanded, the agitation in my voice causing heads to turn.

"You're drawing attention to us. Relax. Sit

down," Enters told me, his eyes demanding my cooperation.

I took a deep breath and sat down. "Okay, but I need some answers and you're not giving them."

"You passed."

I just looked at him, confused.

"With flying colors," he added.

"What are you talking about?"

"We were testing you."

"Testing me," I repeated him, my eyebrows arched.

"We gave you a way out, but you came back."

"And if I had kept going?"

He waved his hand in dismissal of my question. "You didn't."

"But if I had?"

He studied my face for a moment before answering. "Don't be obvious, but take a look at the man at the far corner table, the one wearing the gray sweatshirt."

I looked casually in that direction. It was the man who had arrived in the blue Toyota Camry.

"What about him?"

"He's been trailing you."

"So when I called, you did know who I was?"

"No, not until after.—Oh, by the way, you spent a better night in that tree house then he did across the street." He smiled at me.

"And if I had run?"

"He would have brought you to me."

"And I would have failed."

"Yes."

"I told you I wouldn't run," I reminded him.

"And now I believe you," he replied.

"And if I hadn't gotten out?"

"He would have helped you."

"So that was another test?"

"Yes, another test which you also passed with flying colors. We wanted to know how resourceful you could be, how quickly you could come up with a solution on your own, how quickly you could improvise. What you've proposed to do will require an aptitude for quick thinking."

"So we have a deal?" I asked.

"Mostly. I'm going to help you. I have some ideas. Your plan will be our backup plan. I would prefer to solve this without putting you at risk. I think that's a pretty good deal."

"I agree."

"Good. I'll be leaving now. Enjoy your breakfast. When you're done, walk out and go wait by the Toyota Camry. Jake will meet you there and escort you to a safe place. We mustn't be seen in public together again."

"I understand," I said—and I did. "Will I see you again in a non-public place?"

"Tomorrow. Your first job is to rest, to get your strength back. Tomorrow I'll be by and we'll talk over our strategy."

"Thank you," I told him.

"You're welcome." There was an encouraging smile on his face. I believed in that smile.

A MURDER UNSEEN

Chapter 27

Meeting Candis

Jake was the strong silent type. I had him pegged as such by the time we were 10 minutes into our trip. After the initial greetings, which were cordial, but short, he turned his eyes to the road and didn't say another word. In my mind I had already nicknamed him "The Mute."

Pulling up in front of a high-class apartment complex, he proved he had not gone totally mute on me.

"Ask for Candis McCoy," he instructed in a tired voice as he pulled to a stop, motioning for me to disembark. "You'll be going by the name of Jacqueline Kerns."

"Jacqueline Kerns?"

"That's what I've been told."

I took one look at the fastidiously dressed doorman who stood as erect as a guard and then glanced down at my attire. I turned back to Jake.

"There's no way he'll let me in there."

"What? Of course he will."

I pointed to my attire and Jake's eyebrows raised as he looked at me. For the first time, I think he noticed my dirt-streaked sweatshirt and the generally disheveled condition I was in.

The beginnings of a smile began and then ended abruptly as he looked at my hair. I wondered what I looked like. I was suddenly self-conscious.

"Kyle wasn't thinking? Or is this another test?" I asked wearily.

"No, it's not a test," Jake assured me. "Kyle wasn't thinking. For that matter, neither was I."

He rubbed the bridge of his nose with his thumb and forefinger. It was then that I realized that "The Mute" was exhausted. I had at least slept the night before, even if it hadn't been the best of sleeps. "The Mute" had presumable stood somewhere on the sidewalk across the street watching me. I suddenly felt sorry for him.

"The doorman won't tell a soul. He is as closed-mouth as they come and a long time friend with Candis. However, if another resident sees you that could be a problem."

He put the car back into gear and headed for

the parking lot in back. He parked between a gray Ford Taurus and a red sports car.

"Wait here," he told me as he got out. "I'll go talk with Candis. She'll have a jacket or something you can use."

Jake was back in a few minutes. He handed me a jacket. "Here's a comb too," Jake said next, a wry grin on his face.

I pulled down the sun visor and looked in the mirror, a disgusted look on my face.

"No wonder you've been sour," I told him. "You've had to look at this?" I exclaimed in joking disgust.

"The Mute" even laughed then. The ice was broken.

※※※※※※※※※※

Reaching Candis's apartment door on the fifth floor, I found myself strangely hesitant to knock. I knocked anyway. The door opened, and there was Candis. She was a strikingly beautiful lady in what I guessed was her late fifties or early sixties. A short sophisticated hairstyle was brushed off her face, accentuating her high cheekbones. Her hazel eyes were full of life, warm and welcoming. I felt immediately at ease. Her thin lips parted with a smile as she greeted me, revealing almost perfect teeth.

"Jacqueline, I'm glad you could come. Come on in," she fussed over me, pulling me in, and then locking the door behind me, bolting it. I was glad.

"Thank you for the jacket," I told her simply, handing it back to her.

"Don't think another thing of it," she replied as she eyed me critically. "Child, you look ready to drop. Why don't you go bathe. The bath is running right now, so don't protest. I'll cook up something for you to eat while you freshen up."

She was practically beaming. She was a mother hen clucking over her little chick. It was strangely comforting.

"The bath sounds wonderful," I admitted. "But if I can pass on the food? I just ate at Harvey's."

"How about coffee then?" she asked.

"That sounds wonderful," I responded with a grateful smile.

"Well, let me show you to your room. I trust you can find everything you need there. If I've overlooked something, don't be afraid to holler now," she told me with a smile. "My home is your home." She paused then, something she obviously didn't do too often. "Did Kyle tell you who I am?"

"No, he didn't." I wondered what revelation was about to be unveiled.

"I'm his mother," she told me in a secretive voice.

I looked at her strangely then.

"Oh, McCoy. Yes, my last name is different. No, he didn't disown me and change his name. His father died when Kyle was 12. A hunting accident. I remarried a widower two years later. That's where McCoy comes from.

"Sadly, my second husband died of cancer a few years back, but enough about me. I was going to say that Kyle has filled me in regarding yourself. I trust his judgment implicitly, which means I trust you. You are my guest, not my prisoner, but I would recommend you stay away from the windows, for your own safety."

The words sounded odd rattling off her lips. She was a grandma figure, seeming odd in the role she now played, but I couldn't have asked for a better safe house. I felt at home and I felt safe.

"Now, I have rattled on long enough. Go soak for as long as you wish, and if you decide to pass on the coffee and sleep instead, that's fine with me as well."

"I may end up doing just that," I admitted, suddenly very tired.

"One more thing," she said then, and I smiled inwardly. This woman would always have one more thing to say, but she put me so completely at ease that I couldn't fault her on that.

"There are prescription strength painkillers in the medicine cabinet that Kyle sent over for you, if you need then. There are also some clothes on the bed I set out for you."

She sized me up. "Kyle is pathetic at guessing a woman's clothing size. They will be a bit big, but we can find something that fits better tomorrow.

Until then, at least they are clean."

"They'll be fine," I assured her.

"The bathroom is in here," she told me, hurrying in to shut off the water.

My own private bath. It was sounding better by the minute. I wasn't going to have to feel like I was hogging the bathroom if I soaked for a long time. And soak I did. The bath felt heavenly. It was full and hot, and when at last I finally dragged myself out, wrapping myself in a luxuriously thick, soft towel, I felt human once more.

Slipping into the clean clothes Candis had laid out for me, I towel dried my hair, brushed my teeth, popped the maximum recommended painkillers, and dropped onto the bed, falling instantly asleep. The coffee would have to wait.

I woke to the sound of low voices coming from the living room. Much to my surprise, the noon sun was filtering in through the mini-blinds. I thought I had been sleeping for hours, but a glance at my watch told me it was only twelve-thirty. And then I noticed the date. It was noon—of the next day! I *had* been sleeping for hours!

"How is she?" I recognized Kyle's voice.

"I can't rightly say. She didn't talk much.— Now get that look off your face, Kyle Robert," she protested jovially. "You are right. She didn't get much of a chance to put a word in edgewise with my chattering, but she bathed and then dropped right off to sleep. The poor child was plumb worn out, honey."

"Is that lasagna I smell?" I heard Kyle ask.

"Of course. I made your favorite dish to entice you to stay for lunch."

My stomach told me that I had missed a few meals. I rolled out of bed, feeling refreshed. In the bathroom, I rinsed my mouth with mouthwash, and gave my hair a quick comb through before heading for the door.

"Did we wake you?" Kyle asked as I walked out.

"That, or I woke up and then heard you," I replied with a smile. "I can't believe I slept that long."

"Child, you were exhausted," Candis called from the kitchen. "Sit down and visit while I dish up lunch."

I obliged, sitting down, a smile tugging at the edges of my lips.

"What's so funny?" Kyle asked, his one eyebrow cocked. "Mind letting me in on the joke?"

"Nothing really. Just what your mom said. She's the perfect hostess, putting me so much at ease that I really feel like that's what we are here for right now—to sit and visit."

"She's great. Always has been," Kyle spoke affectionately of his mother.

"You told her everything?" I asked quietly.

"And despite her propensity for chattering, she'll never tell another soul. No one would think she would help me with anything like this.

"She knows your name is Sandra Ford, but we have chosen Jacqueline as your name for now. We needed some alias. Mom always wanted a daughter named Jacqueline."

"I take it she's done this before?"

"She's my best personal safe house when I can't trust the ones the FBI already has. Her record is perfect," he told me with a confident smile. "Better than some of the safe houses we have."

"You're not worried for her?" I asked in a strained voice.

"No. Who would believe she is anything other than what she appears to be? A lovable, congenial, talkative old lady."

"Watch what you say about your mother!" Candis called out, feigning hurt feelings.

I smiled, and then grew serious again.

"But Jake knows," I reminded him.

"Jake doesn't work for the FBI," Kyle told me, smiling broadly.

"There's more to this, isn't there?"

He was still smiling, a glint of humor in his eyes.

"Are you going to let me in on *your* joke?" I asked.

"Jake's my younger brother."

"Your brother.—Do you always drag family

in on your cases?"

"No, we harass him until he lets us have some of the excitement!" Candis exclaimed from the doorway.

"Her hearing is as good as ever," Kyle whispered under his breath.

"I heard that!" Candis warned Kyle.

I laughed.

※※※※※※※※※

The lasagna was delicious, the garlic bread was toasted to perfection, and the salad was crisp and green. The conversation was light and relaxing.

After the table was cleared, and we were sipping on hot coffee, Kyle spoke up.

"Jake did find out one encouraging tidbit so far."

"What would that be?" I asked, a feeling of hope warming me.

"He contacted your old banker, asking him about the money you withdrew, wondering if he knew where it had come from.

"The banker told him that he knew for a fact that it was inheritance money and that he never could figure out why the police had denied that. He said he had even called them about it back then, but they had dismissed him. He says he will testify, if needed."

"You can't let Jake keep investigating. It's not safe. He'll get himself killed," I protested, my voice trembling.

A MURDER UNSEEN

"Jake is a private investigator. He knows how to take of himself," Kyle tried to reassure me.

I shook my head. "No! I would have thought Roger would have known how to take care of himself. Look what happened to him, to his family! I can't let that happen all over again with your family," I told them in a shaky voice. "I...I can't let that happen. Not again."

Candis reached out and took my hands in hers. "We'll be fine. My sons have faced much worse scenarios than this one and come out unscathed. You are safe now. You have to believe that."

"I want to," I told her quietly, "but I'm scared to."

"Do you believe in God?" Candis asked next.

"Yes...," I responded, surprised at the quick change in subject. I was soon to learn that Candis brought God into everything. "In fact, I'm a Christian, though a pretty new one for sure, though I hardly like to admit the fact."

"Are you ashamed?" Candis asked, a perplexed look on her face.

"No, not of God, but of the life I have lived the past year and a half—and the deceitfulness of it."

"God works in wonderful and mysterious ways, Jacqueline. I truly believe He sent you to us right now so we can help you, not simply judicially with your earthly circumstances, but to help you grow to understand more what has taken place in your life. And to think that you are already His child. I was thinking I would get to introduce you to Him, but I can see someone else has already had the privilege."

"Roger did. Well, he showed me the way, but I wasn't ready. Not until two nights ago."

"Oh, you definitely are a newborn babe, aren't you? Well, we'll be taking care of you. God brought you to us for a purpose."

"You are both believers?" I asked.

"All saved by the blood of one very precious Lamb of God," Candis replied, her face alight.

"Welcome to the family," Kyle greeted me into the family of God.

We talked late into the evening of the things of God, and I felt blessed…and loved…and encouraged…and secure. What a new idea after the past year and a half of insecurity. Yet this security wasn't in my circumstances. I knew they could look bleak again. This new found security was in my position before God. I was accepted as perfect by God through His Son, Jesus Christ. I was forgiven. I was His child, and no matter what happened, He would be with me.

A MURDER UNSEEN

Chapter 28

Good News!

It was a few days later, around suppertime, that the two brothers showed up unexpectedly.

"What did you find out?" Candis asked, her eyes bright.

"Coffee first," Jake protested, taking off his jacket and hanging it on the coat rack by the door. He sauntered over to the couch, grinning like the cat that just ate the canary, and sat down.

"Don't feel bad, Mom," Kyle said as he sat down too. "He's not told me a single detail either. All he could do was just grin like that the whole way over here."

I helped Candis serve the coffee, and then we all sat down, waiting expectantly for what news Jake had.

"Okay, what type of luck did you have?" Kyle asked, impatient now.

"Not luck. Talent," Jake insisted, a broad smile on his face.

"No," Candis corrected them both. "God at work." And she smiled at them, knowing they couldn't refute that one.

"I called the State Police in Pennsylvania and obtained a copy of the accident report," Jake began. I knew which accident he was referring to—the one that had been no accident at all!

"The fact that there were scrapes along *both* sides of the vehicle, along with the positioning of the tire tracks, indicated that the vehicle had been *pushed* over the edge—which backs up your version of what happened. I also talked to a retired policeman by the name of Darrel Fritz. Do you remember him?"

"Yes," I replied, nodding my head. "He was the gray-haired detective that was there when I made my report."

"Right. He remembers your report. He described it as 'a murder heard but not seen.' It was the last case he sat in on before he retired the next day. That's why he remembers it. He had brushed it all up to an over-tired, over-worked female. Sorry," Jake said as he glanced in my direction.

"Like I said, that was his last day. He retired,

left the next day on the cruise of his life with his wife of thirty odd years, and by the time he returned it had blown over.

"He hadn't heard anything about it since that night, until I showed up today. He was shocked—and mad. He'll testify that you *did* file the report that they deny ever existed."

Jake had definitely outdone himself in his detective work that day. "The Mute" had also outdone himself on talking that evening. I was impressed, a bit overwhelmed, and joyous.

"Has no one anything to say?" Jake asked.

"Praise the Lord!" Candis whispered in praise.

"Amen to that!" Jake agreed.

I started to cry and laugh at the same time. A miracle was beginning to unfold.

"I'll be approaching my boss with this new information. It gives reasonable doubt on several counts. What I want to do is subpoena all the files on your case and the physical evidence. I want the gun. I want to see if your fingerprints are really on it."

"And...if they are?"

"One step at a time. I'm not so convinced that they are. I think they made that up, planning for a quick closure with no real questions asked because you would be conveniently dead before a trial could be held."

"Then let's pray!" Candis encouraged us. "And tomorrow we'll be praying for you as well."

She took my hand in hers, patting it

reassuringly.

"One day at a time, child. *Be, therefore, not anxious about tomorrow; for tomorrow will be anxious for the things of itself. Sufficient unto the day is its own evil,*" she quoted Matthew 6:34 to me.

"You will have to work on memorizing that verse tomorrow."

"You're right," I agreed.

※※※※※※※※※

Candis was a woman of her word and a woman of prayer. The next day showed me both clearly. We spent the morning in prayer, interspersed with Bible studies as she shared new truths with me. I felt like a dry sponge soaking up each tidbit of truth she lay before me.

The phone rang, just after our noon meal. Candis reached for it. "Hello. This is Candis speaking."

I practically squirmed in my seat, wondering what was being said. Then she frowned, and I panicked inside.

Trust Me. Trust Me. The voice was quiet, non-verbal—but it was definitely speaking to me.

Thank You, Father. I prayed silently as the peace returned. Candis was hanging up. I looked at her, waiting.

"Grandma Garret, not a real Grandma, but an adopted one, fell and broke her hip this morning."

I nearly laughed aloud, my face breaking into

a smile, and then, as suddenly as it came, I was trying to smother it as what she had said hit home. It *wasn't* something to smile about—it's just, I was so relieved! By then Candis was laughing heartily.

"Oh! You poor child! You thought—and I was frowning a furrow as deep as the Grand Canyon across my brow!"

I joined her laughter.

And then the buzzer rang.

"Kyle to see you, Ma'am," the ever-efficient doorman called up.

"Send him up!" Candis responded eagerly.

My hands went to my lips, my eyes closed, and I let out a silent prayer as I waited. Five flights up, even by elevator, gave me plenty of time to pray.

The door opened and Kyle walked in, a broad smile across his normally rather stern looking features.

"No fingerprints!" he nearly shouted, a triumphant ring to his voice.

I ran to him then, tears streaming unabashedly down my cheeks, and hugged him.

"Thank you! Thank you!"

"No. Thank God," Kyle corrected gently, a reverent tone to his voice.

"Thank you, Father," I whispered, my heart turned to Him.

It was over. It was finally over. I could close this chapter of my life forever and begin a new chapter, a new chapter with God.

A MURDER UNSEEN

Chapter 29

Cleared

The charges against me were officially dropped. Calls were exchanged with the police in California. Explanations were given. Details were sent. After reviewing my case, the department agreed to drop the charges against me for the murder of Roger.

Detective Jordan Lewis was arrested and smugly claimed innocence until Cameron Holmes was arrested.

Holmes, when faced with charges of the first degree murder of my family, and four murder attempts on my life, agreed to make a deal. He told everything—and Detective Jordan Lewis's smug smile faded away.

It was discovered that Detective Lewis was part of a national drug ring, as was Detective Graham. For years now, Lewis had been praised for his part in intercepting and catching drug shipments, while all the while he had been allowing the really big ones to slide through undetected.

He was charged with putting out the contract on me and my family. I protested, saying that he was also responsible for the deaths of Roger, Ed, Sally and the boys.

"That can't be proved," the California police had insisted, and so I had to be content with what they could prove.

I mourned my losses, but felt true closure at having Detective Lewis going away for life. I praised the Lord it was over and thanked Him for my newfound friends, for my family in Christ.

The FBI feared retaliation from those in the drug ring, so my newly adopted name of Jacqueline Kerns became permanent.

The new identity bothered me not in the least. I had been changing names regularly since that fatal day several years back now. What was one more?

At least this one was legal. The truth was, I now had a new identity in Christ, and therein was my security.

I was told I could go anywhere I wanted, do anything I wanted. I just had to tell them and they would work out the details.

A MURDER UNSEEN

I decided this time I would move to Florida, just like Henry and I had always planned to do someday. It was a bittersweet moment as I contemplated leaving my newfound friends. It was a daunting thought, one that left me feeling insecure and scared.

Of course, Candis was there with her words of encouragement, reminding me that God would never leave me, and that I was never really alone. She said she would be praying that God would bring some special people into my life to grow me yet more in Him. I believed her.

I reminded myself of all that as I boarded the plane for Florida. My eyes were still moist from the tearful farewell. I had known them for so little a span of time, and yet I already missed them so much. Yet, I can't question the Lord. I can't accuse Him of making a mistake.

"He makes no mistakes." Candis has been pounding that into my brain. She assured me once more of her prayers as she hugged me tightly. Her last words were: "You never know what pleasant surprises the Lord has in store for you. He loves you much more than I am capable of. He'll always be with you."

I knew I shouldn't have, but I felt a nagging doubt at her words. I couldn't fathom pleasant surprises in my near future. I could only envision a quiet, empty house—and the loneliness. And though I knew the Lord would be with me always, my heart and soul yearned for human companionship.

Yet, I was on my way to Florida, mostly because deep within my soul I knew she was right. The Lord is with me and He will sustain me. I've not the foggiest idea how. I can't face tomorrow with all its unknowns. I want security—not unknowns.

I keep quoting that verse in I Corinthians that Candis made sure I memorized: "But my grace is sufficient for you." I continually claim His promises.

※※※※※※※※※

Arriving at the Tallahassee airport, I disembarked the plane, determined to view this as a new adventure, as a new start in life. It wasn't easy though. I was back to where I was before, starting all over again as a stranger in a strange place.

No, you are not being fair, I reprimanded myself. *Yes, I'm a stranger in a strange place, but this time I have a car, a home, and a job. It will be different. I am no longer a fugitive from the law.*

My pep talk was over.

Finding my new car was easy. A blue Toyota Camry. I had always wanted one, and this time the government was paying.

Finding my new home wasn't quite as easy. I missed the exit off the freeway and had to drive around for a while to find my way back—but I did find it in the end. And here I am, pulling into my own driveway, into my own garage. Leaning back against the seat, I have to smile. This is my home.

A MURDER UNSEEN

For better or for worse, I am home.

Turning off the ignition, I get out of the car slowly, surveying my surroundings. No, surveying is not the right word. I'm soaking in my surroundings. I'm home.

Through the back door of the garage I can see the yard. It is all I asked for and more. The lawn is lush green, the flower gardens bring color and life, and a patio set beckons me to come. But not yet. I want to see inside.

Suddenly I'm a child again. It's Christmas. I want to unwrap my present. I want to see my home, and in seeing it, making it mine. I head for the door.

It is then that I notice the door is slowly opening. My heart constricts. Blood pounds in my head like a freight train. I want to scream, but nothing will come out! I can barely breathe in my terror.

They are here! They have found me! The horrifying thoughts race through my petrified mind, snapping me out of my state of shock.

I dive for the passenger's door of the car, glad the keys are still in my hand.

"Pamela!" I hear my name. More than that, I hear a voice calling me from the grave, a voice calling me by the name he knows me best.

My head turns slowly, in disbelief, toward the sound of that voice. I stare, mouth agape, in shock once more, at the face of Roger!

"Pamela," he says my name once more,

gently, comfortingly.

"Roger!" The name finally stumbles out of my mouth. Suddenly I'm embarrassed, realizing how dumbfounded I look, realizing how unladylike I must appear, sprawled as I am on the front seat of the car in my desperate attempt to escape my assailants.

"I...I thought you were dead.—Right now I...I thought you were them.—What happened?" The questions spurt out of my mouth.

Finding it impossible to wipe the dumbfounded look off my face, I somehow manage to upright myself and climb back out of the car, regaining some of my dignity. Roger is walking down the steps now, his arms outstretched.

"You're alive!" I exclaim, shaking.

My eyes dart nervously from him to the door. Will someone come bursting through those doors? Is this really happening? Are we safe?

"Pamela, relax," he says then, his arms enveloping me. "You're safe."

"I'm safe," I repeat him, as though the repetition itself will make it be so. "I'm safe."

"Yes, you are safe." He smiles down at me. His hand lovingly brushes my hair back from my eyes.

"You're alive," I say again. A broken record. I'm still in mild shock.

"Yes, I'm alive," he reassures me.

"But the death report?"

"Are you doubting my existence?" he teases

me, his eyes laughing.

I get that first inkling of real hope. We're joking again like old times. Maybe everything will be okay.

"I faked my death with some help from friends in high places," Roger explains.

"Why?"

"Because you convinced me you were right. I figured I was safer dead than alive—and of more help to you that way. The problem was that, after you took off, I couldn't find you.

"I ran background checks on Detective Graham and Lewis. Lewis was as clean as a whistle. Too clean really. It's like he was working overtime at protecting himself. But Detective Graham had a few black marks. Nothing serious on their own, but putting two and two together, I could see bad cop written all over him.

"After the fact, I heard of your arrest. Kyle and Jake had already put together a great defense on your behalf. My testimony didn't hurt your case any."

"So Kyle and Jake knew you were alive?" I ask, a light coming on in my head.

"And Candis," Roger admits.

"You never know what pleasant surprises the Lord has in store for you," I quote Candis, smiling and shaking my head. Roger is looking at me oddly.

"Candis.—That's what she told me when I left New York," I explain.

"Okay, the light comes on," Roger replies.

"Did you speak with them?"

"Enough to know that you are a believer," Roger answers me, his eyes glowing.

"Yes, I'm a believer now," I tell him, basking in his closeness, but not understanding it.

"So you're not mad at me?" I ask cautiously.

"Mad at you?" his voice is incredulous. "Whatever for?"

"For shooting you!" I exclaim.

His laugh was deep. And real. "My poor little Pamela, how could you believe that I would hold that against you?"

"Why shouldn't you?" I ask, scared to believe that things could mend so easily.

"Because I love you."

"You love me?" I question him, my eyes searching his.

"I was hoping you would reciprocate," he says then, a twinkle in his eyes.

"Reciprocate," I repeat him dumbly.

"Well, it's hard to ask someone to marry you if they don't love you," he explains in a serious tone of voice, but his eyes are still twinkling.

"Yes, that would be a problem," I admit in an equally serious tone, my face a blank.

"Is it a problem for us?" he asks, all seriousness now, and not without a spark of uncertainty in his eyes.

"No, it's not a problem," I answer him at

length, a smile beginning in the corner of my mouth and growing to envelope my face at the realization that the obstacles are gone. All the things that held me back are now of no importance. Closure on my past has come.

I open my mouth to express my love—but then a shadow crosses my face. Sally and her family. My closure is not complete. Can Roger ever really forgive me for putting his sister and her family in harm's way, resulting in their deaths?

"What's wrong?" Roger asks.

"What about your sister and her family? Can you really forgive me for getting them involved in all this? For getting them killed?"

"Killed? I'm the farthest thing from dead!" The voice comes from the doorway to the backyard.

"Would you please just go ahead and say you'll marry him so we can all come in and I can hug you like there's no tomorrow?"

"Sally?"

"Alive and well and in the flesh."

Suddenly I was being swarmed by Kendra and the twins. Ed is standing behind Sally, his arm wrapped protectively around her—and then we're in a group hug.

Everyone is talking all at once. Explanations of the necessity of their presumed deaths are explained in spurts between the tears of a joyful reunion intermingled with bursts of laughter. I catch enough between Kendra's squeals of delight and the twins tugging at my pant legs to know an attempt on their lives had been made, and that Roger had engineered the failed attempt into an apparent successful one—one in which his sister's family then disappeared off the radar into a quiet existence in western Canada while Roger continued to investigate my case.

They are alive. I am not responsible for their deaths. Roger kept his word. He protected them. Closure is complete.

I turn to Roger. Amidst the hub-hub of our reunion he is waiting, waiting for an answer.

"I love you, Roger," I mouth the words in his direction as my eyes connect with his. And then I'm in his arms and for a few seconds I'm oblivious to the pandemonium around me. *Thank You, Lord!*

And to think I had envisioned a quiet, empty house—and loneliness.

To order additional copies of
A Murder Unseen
Visit any of the websites below:
www.createspace.com/3618322
www.amazon.com
www.booksbyrosie.net

Betrayed
by Rosie Cochran

While on assignment to uncover the details of an assassination plot, Jeremi Grant sustains a gunshot wound that grazes his skull, leaving him with no memory. An undercover FBI agent is dead. His fellow agents want the man who did it. All evidence points to Jeremi.

Under arrest for murder, Jeremi has no explanation for the FBI. Worse yet, he has no explanation for himself. He struggles to reconcile between the evidence laid before him and the man he feels he is inside.

Meanwhile, an assassination is going to take place and the details needed to prevent it are locked in Jeremi's mind. Escaping from the FBI, Jeremi is determined to find out who he really is. The joy of remembering that he is a Christian is dampened by questions over his many dubious talents. Who and what was he? The pieces slowly begin to fall into place, but will Jeremi remember enough, soon enough, in order to prevent the assassination?

Available at:

www.amazon.com
www.booksbyrosie.net
www.winepressbooks.com

Identity Revealed
by Rosie Cochran

Can one hide forever under witness protection? What if there is a leak? What happens then?

These thoughts have tormented Alyssa. She's about to find out what happens when her nightmares become reality. She's about to find out if her God is real enough to carry her through.

Identity Revealed is the sequel to **Betrayed!**

Available at:
www.createspace.com/3360541
www.amazon.com
www.booksbyrosie.net

Made in the USA
Middletown, DE
03 December 2015